KEEPING QUIET

Other titles by Penny Kendal

Broken
Christina's Face
The Weekend Ghost

For more information about Penny Kendal's books see:
www.pennykendal.co.uk

KEEPING QUIET

PENNY KENDAL

Andersen Press • London

For my grandmother, Cynthia Kendal

First published in 2005 by
Andersen Press Limited,
20 Vauxhall Bridge Road, London SW1V 2SA
www.andersenpress.co.uk

British Library Cataloguing in Publication Data available
ISBN 1 84270 455 9

Typeset by FiSH Books, Enfield, Middlesex
Printed and bound in Great Britain by
Bookmarque Ltd., Croydon, Surrey

Chapter 1

When you see something bad, you want to tell someone, right? And I wanted to tell someone – honest, I did.

I was down by the canal when I saw them – a man and a woman, further along, by some old sheds. They were yelling at each other. That may not sound like much but the man's voice was grainy and vicious. It made me shudder. I was too far away to hear the exact words, but there was definitely a lot of swearing and it was strong stuff.

I ducked back behind a twiggy bush and peered out. It wasn't dark but it was starting to get that way so I couldn't see too clearly. The man had his back to me which didn't help. All I could make out was his white neck sticking out between a black jacket and black beanie hat. The woman was Asian and she looked younger; she had a long grey coat and red scarf and she was hugging herself like she was trying to keep warm. Anyway, he started pushing at her. Then he hit her and she screamed. She tried to hit him back and he got hold of her but she wouldn't give up and they were fighting.

Maybe you've seen stuff like that before, but I haven't. It was weird, like I was watching it on TV; like it couldn't really be happening. I mean, I've seen it in the playground, of course – Sean Finch – he's the top fighter in my year. I keep well away from him. But it's usually only boys. I've never seen a man and a woman fighting like that.

1

I watched them and they were getting closer and closer to the edge – it looked like they were both going to end up in the canal. It was January and freezing cold. I was shivering enough just standing there; that water would be like ice. But the woman must have realised and she managed to wriggle out of his grip. She moved away from the edge and he waved his arms about threateningly and started yelling at her again.

I didn't know what to do. I wanted to shout at them to stop but there was no way I had the guts. I looked to see if anyone else was around. I was the only one.

I know what you're thinking – 'But, Michael, didn't you have a mobile phone? Couldn't you have rung the police or something?' I did have a mobile but it was a bit manky since I spilt Tango on it. It still worked sometimes; it was just kind of sticky. I only had it for emergencies. And I suppose you could say this was an emergency, only I didn't know that at the time – not for sure. Anyway, I'd forgotten to charge it up and the battery was flat. Okay? So I couldn't have used it, even if I'd wanted to.

I stayed there, watching as the man shouted and the woman shouted back. Then he hit her again. She cried out, trying to shield her face with her arms.

I winced. I was scared for her – but I was also scared that the man might look round any moment and see me. The bare bushes were not giving me much cover. What if he decided to turn on me? And I couldn't bear to watch any longer. So I went – through the gap into Crawford Road. I was only three minutes from home. I wanted to tell Mum or Dad or even Jamie. They'd know what to do – they'd know if we ought to call the police or anything.

When I got home I had my mouth open, bursting to tell someone the second I got through the door. But Mum must've had her mouth open too because she got in first.

'Michael! Where've you been? You're late.'

I told her I had detention and she frowned. 'I thought you're supposed to be given notice for a detention?'

'Sorry – I didn't get a chance to tell you yesterday. Mum – I need to tell you something now – something I...'

'It'll have to wait till later. I've got enough on my plate right now. Jamie's lost the music for his rehearsal tonight – Stravinsky's *Firebird Suite*. Have you seen it, Michael?'

She said it like it must be my fault. Like I must have done something with Jamie's music. I glared at her.

'I'm not blaming you, Michael. I'm only asking.'

I shook my head.

'Well you can at least help look for it, now you're here.'

'But, Mum...I've got to tell you...'

'Michael, *not now*.' She ran her fingers through her hair like she does when she's stressed out. Then she turned and went upstairs.

I followed her up, thinking if she wasn't going to listen to me, maybe Jamie would. I should've known better. I only had to look at him to see there was no chance. Jamie was pacing up and down like a tormented zoo animal.

'It must be somewhere,' he was saying. 'A piece of music can't disappear. It can't decide it feels like a holiday and book a flight to the Caribbean, can it?'

He looked at me. I shook my head.

Jamie thumped the wall. 'It's only the second rehearsal. What's Mr Minton going to say if I turn up without my music? And I wanted to practise again before I go. Help me, Michael – please!' He got down on his knees, with his hands together like he was praying. He can be a bit overdramatic sometimes, my brother.

So before I knew it I was helping to look for Jamie's music. Jamie was still going mad about it and Dad wasn't home. Mum was in a right state. And I'd said nothing about what I saw.

I know – you're thinking, wasn't what I saw more important than some lost sheet music? Well, not in our house. In our house Jamie's music is the most important thing in the world. You see, my brother Jamie is a genius – a musical genius.

It's not surprising that one of us is musical. Mum and Dad are both professional musicians: Mum plays the viola and Dad plays the violin. What's more surprising is that one of us *isn't* musical. Yes – you guessed it – that's me.

Jamie's eleven. He keeps his room tidy, not like mine, so I don't know how he'd managed to lose his music. But he'd just got into this top youth orchestra so I could understand why he was upset.

I tried looking in the music room. And don't start

thinking we're posh because we've got a music room – it's the spare bedroom with a few music stands and a piano, that's all. So I was looking in there even though Jamie said he'd already searched every inch of it. But I was still thinking about what I saw.

I should've said something, I know I should. But it was just two people fighting – that's all – it was none of my business. It's the kind of thing that happens all the time, doesn't it? Only not usually round here, in Thurbridge, not during the day.

I thought about trying again – to tell Mum. And then I realised. If I said anything Mum would have to know that I was down by the canal. It's a shortcut home from school and she's told me enough times not to go that way. It's only because she thinks I'll fall in and I can't swim. Yeah – I know, I'm thirteen and I can't swim. There's no need to laugh – I'll explain in a minute. I don't come home by the canal all the time, but it's miles quicker and I stay right away from the edge.

Mum was in a bad enough mood as it was; she would have gone ape if she'd known I was down by the canal! So then, I'm glad I never said anything. And I can't believe I didn't think of it before. Anyway, by now that fight would have been over ages ago and they'd be long gone.

Then Dad came home. When he heard about Jamie's music his face went kind of guilty looking. He didn't say a word. He lifted his briefcase onto the kitchen table and opened it. He started flicking through papers.

Jamie watched with his eyes bulging. 'Dad...you didn't?'

'Hang on,' Dad mumbled, 'one sec – it rings a bell, that's all.'

Then Dad's hands stopped. He pulled out a piece of music. 'Here! I thought I'd seen it.' He held it out, with his head bowed. 'I'm so sorry, Jamie. You must've left it on the music stand and I picked it up with mine.'

Jamie had a few choice words for Dad, and so did Mum. 'Do you know how long we've been looking?' was just the beginning.

Luckily for Dad, Jamie was in a rush to get to his rehearsal and Mum had to take him. She was going straight on to play in a concert, so Dad rustled up a Chinese stir-fry for the two of us. We ate, and I thought about saying something to Dad. He wouldn't have thrown a wobbly about the canal, like Mum, but there didn't seem much point. It all felt kind of distant by then. I wanted to push it out of my mind, like it hadn't really happened.

So I said nothing. Well, I didn't say nothing exactly, just nothing about what I saw. Instead I went on at Dad about the unfairness of Miss Fowler giving me detention. She shouldn't pick on me just because I've got messy writing. It's not my fault. I've got trouble with my co-ordination – dyspraxia, it's called. It means I'm no good at football and swimming and handwriting and that kind of stuff. Most teachers are understanding but not Miss Fowler.

Dad was sympathetic but then he had to go and pick Jamie up so I got on with my French homework. When they came back, Jamie did his homework while I watched TV with Dad, until it was time to go to bed.

In the morning, when I got up, Jamie was already

practising on his violin, as usual. You don't know what I have to put up with – violins and violas every second of the day. And Mum was nagging me to hurry up, because I'm always a bit slow getting dressed.

Then we had breakfast and Jamie rushed through his because he wanted to get another quick violin practice in before school. Dad was off to play in concert in Newcastle for three days and he was in a rush too. So Mum asked me to clear the table. When I was little I was never allowed to do it because I was always dropping things but I'm better now, and this is the *amazing* reward. I get to clear the table!

The radio was on in the kitchen. It was the local news, though no one was really listening. I was carrying a plate and mug towards the dishwasher. That's when I heard it – '*and finally, the body of a woman has been found in the canal near Thurbridge.*'

I managed to hold onto the plate. But the mug went crashing to the floor.

Chapter 2

I stood there in a daze. I don't even know if they said any more about it on the radio because Mum turned it off and started harping on at me about being more careful.

'*Mum* . . .' I began. I wanted to tell her what I'd heard – and what I'd seen yesterday. But I wasn't sure. My head was all muddled. I needed to think.

Mum didn't hear me anyway. She had her head in a cupboard. She stood up, holding out a dustpan and brush.

'I haven't got time . . .' I protested.

'Nor have I,' said Mum. 'And it's your mess, so you can clean it up.'

That was it. She clearly wasn't going to listen to me. There was no point in trying to tell her anything.

I crouched down and started sweeping the pieces into the pan. I'm not a good aim at the best of times and I was feeling all shaky, so some bits went flying under the fridge.

'Give it to me,' Mum said angrily. 'Go on – get off to school.'

'I'm sorry, Mum,' I said.

'All right – I know it was an accident. Go on – off you go.'

I walked the long way round to school. I wasn't going

near that canal, even if I was late. My head was spinning like I'd been on one of those fairground rides. Maybe it wasn't her, I told myself. Just because they found a body – didn't mean it was the same woman, did it? But what if it was? And it was my fault she was dead, because I'd seen that fight and I hadn't called the police, or told anyone – or done anything about it at all?

When I got to school the playground was empty. I went up to my form room. The door was open and from the noise I could tell Mrs Deakin wasn't there yet. Phew. At least I wouldn't get a late mark. As I walked in the noise stopped – everyone was staring at me. I looked down to check my flies and to make sure half my breakfast wasn't down my shirt. It wasn't that. What was going on?

'They know,' I suddenly thought. 'They know I saw that fight and didn't tell anyone. They know some woman's dead because of me.' But they couldn't know, could they?

I walked nervously towards my seat. It was only when I turned round that I saw Shamila. She must've come in right behind me. It was her everyone had been staring at – not me. She's pretty, Shamila – worth a stare any day. Sometimes I can't take my eyes off her. But everyone doesn't usually stare at her like that – all at once. I stared. She wasn't looking so pretty today. Her mouth was turned down and her eyes looked kind of hollow.

Shamila sat down. People started whispering.

'What's going on?' I asked Liam.

But at that moment Mrs Deakin appeared, looking flustered. 'I'm sorry I'm late – I had trouble with the car.

Well done all of you for waiting so sensibly. Let's keep it quiet now for the register.'

'Tell me, Liam,' I whispered.

Mrs Deakin looked up, straight at me. I'm not too good at whispering – it must've come out louder than I thought. Mrs Deakin raised her eyebrows and smiled. She's all right, she is. She's been my form tutor since Year Seven.

She looked back down at the register. I looked at Liam.

'Later,' Liam mouthed.

'Well?' I asked Liam again. We were in the corridor walking to English. 'What was going on when I came in?'

'Did you hear about that body – the one they found in the canal?' said Liam.

I stopped – causing a pile-up behind me as everyone lunged into each other.

'Wh... what about it?'

'It was Shamila's cousin.'

'*What?* How do you know?'

'Selen in our class – she walks to school with a girl in Year Ten, whose nan lives next door to Shamila. This girl's nan saw the police go round there and everything.'

'That's just rumours,' I pointed out. 'You don't know for sure.'

'But you saw Shamila,' said Liam. 'It must be true.'

I didn't want it to be true. I badly didn't want it to be true. But I *had* seen Shamila.

'Do you know when they found the body?' I asked.

Liam shrugged. 'If you want the gory details you'll have to ask Shamila.'

I baulked in horror. 'I can't.'

'You can try asking Selen if you like,' said Liam.

But Selen isn't in my English class – or Shamila, so I had no chance to find out anymore before break.

I hardly got a thing done in English. I couldn't stop thinking about the woman – standing on the bank in her grey coat. Now she was dead. How could I know the man was going to push her in the canal and leave her to die? I mean if I'd thought that was going to happen I'd have called the police for sure, wouldn't I? I know that fight looked bad – but I didn't think it was *that* bad.

If I'd known it was Shamila's cousin, that would have been different too – but the woman was a complete stranger – they both were. It was nothing to do with me. I blame Miss Fowler. If she hadn't given me that detention I wouldn't have been late out of school. I wouldn't have been there. I wouldn't have seen. And I did try to tell Mum, didn't I? If it wasn't for Jamie and his stupid music, she would have listened to me. So it was Mum's fault too – and Jamie's – and Miss Fowler's – not just mine.

I thought maybe I should go to the police, after school – tell them what I saw. But they'd want to know why I hadn't told them yesterday. And it wasn't as if I could describe the man or anything – I only saw him from the back. I couldn't help – so there was no point, was there? And of course there was Shamila – I couldn't bear the idea of Shamila knowing what I saw, knowing I might've been able to do something, and her cousin might still be alive, if it wasn't for me.

*

11

At break I looked for Selen but I didn't find her. It was Shamila I found. Not on purpose – I almost walked into her. She was standing on her own near the cloakrooms. She looked like she might've been crying.

Now, you've got to understand that Shamila is way out of my league. She's beautiful, right, not the kind of girl who would look twice at me. I'd never even talked to her before – not properly.

So I was standing there – it was me and Shamila – and my tongue was in knots. It took me ages to untie it enough to get some words out. 'Shamila . . . are you okay?' I asked.

She looked at me, kind of scathing-like. 'Michael, do I look okay?'

There was bitterness in her voice that I'd never heard before. She must have saved it specially for me.

I didn't know what to say. But she wasn't moving and nor was I, so I had to try again. 'I'm sorry – listen, I heard about your cousin. Is it true?'

Shamila nodded slowly. 'I can't understand how everyone knew – even before I got to school.'

'I can tell you that,' I said. 'Liam told me. It was Selen in our class – she walks to school with a girl in Year Ten, whose nan lives next door to you. This girl's nan saw the police go round and everything.'

'Oh,' said Shamila.

'How come you're on your own?' I asked awkwardly. 'Where's your friends?'

'I think they're avoiding me. They don't know what to say. They'd rather gossip amongst themselves.'

She had that same bitter tone for her friends – so it wasn't just me. That was something.

'I'm surprised you've come to school, with all that happening,' I said. 'I shouldn't think you can concentrate much.'

I knew how I'd been in English. It must have been even worse for her.

Shamila spoke almost in a whisper. 'Mum and Dad had to go with the police. I think they must've needed them to identify the body. Dad thought it'd be better for me to come to school, keep things normal, rather than hanging around at home. I think they wanted me out of the way. And they didn't think anyone at school would know.'

'So it might not be your cousin? It's not definite?' I said hopefully.

Shamila shook her head. 'I know it's her though. Dad went and reported her missing when she wasn't home at one this morning. She always phones if she's going to be late. He knew something must have happened. But the police said she's eighteen and she'd probably gone off somewhere with some friends. They wouldn't do anything. Dad was going spare. He feels responsible you see. When Neeta got into Uni down here, Mum and Dad said she could live with us, because accommodation's so expensive compared to up North.'

'So... when did they find the body then?' I asked.

'About six this morning – a man was walking across Gorton Bridge when he thought he saw something floating in the water.'

Tears began to seep down Shamila's face. I panicked. I reached into my pocket for a tissue. I wanted to wipe her tears away. I wanted the crying to stop. I couldn't

13

bear it. *It's my fault – my fault*, that was all I could think, over and over.

The only tissue I could find looked a bit well used. I pushed it quickly back in my pocket. 'I haven't got a tissue – not a clean one,' I muttered. 'I'm sorry.'

Shamila wiped her face on her sleeve. 'It's so awful,' she said. 'Neeta – she's such a kind, lovely girl.'

'She *was*, you mean,' I said.

Shamila stared at me.

'I didn't . . . I mean,' I mumbled. I'd really put my foot in it now.

Shamila's tears started up again. I felt like crying myself.

It was then that three girls came round the corner – Shamila's friends. When they saw us they started squawking like a bunch of starlings.

'Shamila! Where've you been? We were looking all over for you. What are you doing with *him*? Has he been upsetting you? What've you been saying, Michael? Leave her alone. *Go on*.'

There was no point in arguing. Too many of them – and they were right – I'd only been upsetting Shamila. I know – I'm gutless, I admit it.

I walked along the corridor and in my mind I was back there, by the canal. I see the man and the woman – the fight, only instead of running off home I shout out, 'Oy you! Stop that!' And my voice is loud and deep, so I sound like I mean business. And it's the man who's running home, not me – and the woman's sobbing and I put my arm round her shoulder and she says, 'Thank you – Oh thank you. You've saved my life.' And I meet her

14

eyes – only it's not Shamila's cousin – it's Shamila, and those deep, dark eyes are full of ... full of *love* ...

'*Michael! You stupid clumsy boy!*'

I'd only gone and walked right into Miss Fowler. The pile of papers she'd been carrying was scattered over the floor and she was rubbing her arm.

'What on earth were you doing? Walking about with your eyes shut? At least help me pick this lot up. And, Michael, you'd better take that scowl off your face if you don't want another detention.'

The scowl on my face was not keen to move. But I didn't want detention – not again. So I found myself down on the floor, trying to clear up the mess I'd made. Sounds familiar, right?

Chapter 3

I tried to find Shamila at lunchtime. It wasn't easy because I was trying to avoid Sean Finch at the same time. We'd had P.E. before lunch – volleyball, and I'd accidentally trodden on Sean's foot. It had to be him, didn't it? Mr Muscleman himself. Like I didn't have enough to worry about.

'Shamila, where are you?' I muttered, edging nervously round the science block. Our school site is that big you can get lost in it for days – well, hours, anyway. I know because in my first week here I got lost about twelve times. And since Jamie started here last September I've only bumped into him twice! Mind you, I don't think he ever comes out of the music block.

I spied Sean kicking a ball about with his gang and ducked back round the corner. Phew – he didn't see me. That was lucky. He's not one to mess with, Sean. If it'd been him at the canal yesterday I bet he'd have punched that man's lights out. Mind you, maybe he wouldn't – not for an Asian girl. He's a right racist, he is.

I kept looking for Shamila but I couldn't find her. I didn't see her until I was in the dinner queue. She was sitting with her mates and there was no getting near her. She wouldn't meet my eyes. I couldn't bear that I'd upset her. I was desperate to apologise to her. But I needed to get her on her own. I wasn't about to do it with her mates listening in.

I sat down with Darren and Nick, a few tables away.

I'd thought I was hungry but now I couldn't eat a thing. I could see Shamila wasn't eating either.

'Aren't you eating that?' Darren was eyeing my plate greedily, having already polished off his own. His stomach's like a bottomless pit. It's easy to see why he's not much cop at football.

'Here – it's all yours.' I pushed it towards him.

'Hey, you're not getting that anorexia, are you?' said Nick.

'I'm not hungry, that's all,' I told him.

'Something must be up,' Nick insisted. 'It's not like you.'

Darren grinned. 'It's a girl,' he said. 'It's one of them – over there. He hasn't stopped looking that way since he sat down. I'm right, aren't I, Michael?'

I knew my face was going red. I tried to stop looking at Shamila.

'Come on, tell us then – which one is it?' said Darren. 'Bet it's Kelly? I can tell you now, you've got no chance.'

'Leave it out, will you,' I told them. 'I'm going outside.'

Darren and Nick can be dead irritating sometimes.

I couldn't get near Shamila all afternoon. It was after school when I finally, *finally* got my chance. She came out on her own – right in front of me.

'Shamila!' I called.

She turned.

'I...I...err...' I stumbled.

'What, Michael?'

'I...I'm so sorry about what I said this morning. Me and my big mouth – I know I said the wrong thing. I only wanted to help, that's all.'

17

'Don't worry about it,' she said. Her dark eyelashes fluttered and I felt my face hotting up. 'It's not you, Michael – it's me. I don't know how I can bear it! I feel like it's all my fault.'

'*Your fault?*' I repeated. What could she mean? Had she seen the fight too?

'I knew how depressed Neeta was,' said Shamila. 'She tried two weeks ago, you see. I should have known – maybe I could have talked her out of it. And she made me promise not to tell Mum and Dad. I shouldn't have promised – or I should have told them anyway...'

'What are you on about?' I asked, confused. 'What did she try two weeks ago?'

Shamila met my eyes, clearly puzzled that I didn't understand. Her face was full of pain. 'Suicide,' she said. 'Neeta tried to kill herself two weeks ago. This time she's done it.'

Suicide. My mouth hung open in shock. Before I could get myself together enough to speak, Shamila was looking towards a car that had pulled up over the road. 'That's my mum's car – she's come to pick me up – I'll have to go. 'Bye, Michael.'

''Bye...' I called but she was already too far away to hear. I stood staring after her until the car disappeared out of sight.

I started walking. 'What could it mean? Maybe it was a different woman. The one I saw might have been long gone when another woman came along and chucked herself in the canal. Or the man could have gone off and the woman was so upset about whatever it was they were rowing about that she thought suicide was the only way out. *Or,*

Shamila could be wrong and it wasn't suicide at all.

I found myself heading towards the canal. I didn't want to but I had to look – to see the scene again. I slowed down as I got nearer. My heart was beating fast. I somehow expected to see police all over the place and fluorescent tape. But there was nothing – nothing to say anything had happened there at all. Just bunches of kids walking home from school, like they do every day.

I stepped onto the path – but I couldn't go any further. The dark water looked so threatening. Someone had died here. Someone had been alive this time yesterday and now they were dead. My stomach was heaving. Why did I feel so guilty? None of it was my fault, whatever had happened – was it? I turned to walk back the long way home.

'Forgotten something, Mickey?'

It was Sean Finch.

I wished now that I hadn't turned back. Walking along the canal would be better than a going-over from Sean Finch. Mind you, I was still too near the water for my liking. What if Sean decided I needed a ducking?

'L-left my maths book,' I told him nervously. 'Need it for homework.'

I was trying hard not to look at his foot – the one I'd trodden on earlier. He could tell.

'Think I'm going to get mad because Mickey Mouse trod on my foot?' he said, sneering. 'There's people out there that need sorting – but not you, Mickey, mate. You're lucky though – that foot's scored more goals for our team than any other foot in the school. If you were a heavyweight instead of a feather, things might've been different.'

I nodded, trying not to show my relief. I'm no feather-weight but I wasn't going to argue with him. 'Well, gotta go. See-ya.'

I hurried off. I was so distracted I found myself back at the school gates before I remembered that I didn't need my maths book. That was only an excuse I'd made up for Sean.

I clutched my head in frustration and kicked the gatepost. Then my heart sank. Mrs Deakin was walking towards the admin block and had seen me. She hurried over, looking worried.

'Are you all right, Michael?'

'Yes, fine,' I said lamely. My mind was blank. I couldn't think of an excuse.

She came closer. 'If you ever want to talk to me about anything, you know I'm always ready to listen.'

I nodded, cringing with embarrassment. I like Mrs Deakin but I didn't want her fussing over me. She must have thought I was being bullied and was too scared to walk home or something.

'Thanks, Miss,' I said. 'I'd better get home now.'

I set off. I had to pull myself together, get things straight in my mind. The thing was, I told myself, if Shamila's cousin Neeta had killed herself, then the police wouldn't be looking for witnesses. And I didn't actually witness it anyway, whether it was suicide or not. There was no reason to say anything to anyone about what I'd seen. The best thing was to forget it – and get on with my life. I would say nothing to no one. Nothing.

Chapter 4

Mum opened the door to me, cheerfully. 'I wondered where you'd got to. Wasn't detention again, was it?'

'No,' I said. 'I was a bit late out, that's all.'

'Well, your dad's still in Newcastle and Jamie's at his violin lesson so I thought we could sit down and have a proper chat, just the two of us. I know you've been wanting to talk to me and I haven't had time, but you know how things are... Anyway – I have time now. Shall I put the kettle on?'

I shrugged. Mum headed for the kettle. I took off my coat and sat down at the kitchen table, bewildered. I was surprised she'd even noticed that I'd been trying to tell her something the day before. It would have been a whole lot better if she'd had time to listen then. If Jamie hadn't had to take her over completely like always.

Mum pushed a cup of tea towards me.

'Biscuits?' she asked.

I shook my head. I was hungry – I hadn't had lunch, but I was so tensed up, if I tried to eat anything I would choke. She sat down opposite. I psyched myself up. I knew then that I was going to tell her everything. What I'd decided – about saying nothing, telling no one, had gone out the window. It was all about to come pouring out.

'Mum...' I began.

She smiled reassuringly. 'Your dad's told me something about it,' she said.

I frowned. What did she mean?

'We can't have you getting detentions when it's not your fault,' she went on. 'Who is this Miss Fowler? I don't remember you mentioning her before. I thought Mr Barnaby was your maths teacher. I want you to tell me all about it, Michael.'

I took a deep breath – and I told her. No – not about the fight and Shamila's cousin. About Miss Fowler. Yes, I know, I chickened out. Slagging off Miss Fowler was a much easier option when it came down to it.

'Mr Barnaby's taken two terms off to look after his baby,' I began. 'His wife earns more than him so she's gone back to work and we got landed with Miss Fowler. Worst luck.'

'So what's been going on with this Miss Fowler?' said Mum.

'She hates me,' I grumbled. 'She's always picking on me. She says I work too slowly and my book's too messy to mark.'

'Doesn't she know about your dyspraxia?' Mum asked.

I shrugged.

'Haven't you told her?' Mum continued. 'When she complains about your work, haven't you tried explaining to her?'

'*Mum*, you don't know what it's like.'

'Oh, Michael,' Mum sighed. 'In that case I'm going round to that school tomorrow to set them straight. That Miss Fowler should have been told. It's not your job or mine to tell her.'

'No way, Mum! You can't do that!'

'Michael – I'm trying to make things better for you.'

Make things better. If only she could. Like make yesterday never happen, make Shamila's cousin still alive.

'I don't want you going into school,' I insisted. 'I'll be a laughing stock if anyone sees you.'

'Ashamed of me, are you?'

'It's not the done thing to have your mum walking round school, that's all.'

'I'll phone then,' said Mum.

'If you must.' I stood up.

'You haven't drunk your tea,' she said.

'I've got homework to do.'

I grabbed some biscuits from the tin and went upstairs.

At least I hadn't tried to tell her about the fight by the canal. That was definitely the right decision. The way she'd gone on at me about Miss Fowler, I'm sure she'd have had me straight down to the police station – even if I told her Shamila said it was suicide. Mum interrogating me was bad enough – but the police would be something else. And it wasn't as if I could tell them anything useful, anyway. They'd probably have me up for wasting police time.

23

Chapter 5

The next day was Friday. Shamila wasn't in school. I wasn't exactly surprised, but I was disappointed. I'd wanted to talk to her again, to find out more. I'd wanted to see her.

Without Shamila there, everyone was talking about it freely – they didn't have to keep to hushed whispers. Word had got round that it was suicide. I'm not sure how.

'Why does anyone kill themselves, anyway?' asked Kelly, in registration. 'I think it's a sin – and it's selfish too. Look at the state Shamila was in yesterday. Her cousin didn't think about how her family would feel, did she, Miss?'

Mrs Deakin looked up, a pained frown on her face.

'I know it's hard to understand,' she said, finally, 'but sometimes a person can become ill, with depression or another kind of mental illness. They feel like life is unbearable.'

'So d'you reckon Shamila's cousin was a nutter then?' asked Liam.

Mrs Deakin flinched at the word, shaking her head firmly. 'That's not a nice expression, Liam. She may have been ill. I don't know. No one knows. It's very sad, that's all I can say.'

'But if she wanted to die – shouldn't she be allowed to do what she wants?' I asked.

Everyone turned to look at me – including Mrs Deakin,

a worried stare on her face. What had I done? Why did I say that? Now, not only did she think I was being bullied; she probably thought I was suicidal as well.

'That's ... an interesting question, Michael,' she said. She opened her mouth to continue but at the same moment the bell rang for first lesson. Chairs scraped as everyone gathered their things.

'It's sinful,' said Kelly.

Mrs Deakin closed the register and stood up. 'Something for you to think about, anyway,' she said.

I, for one, couldn't stop thinking about it. I didn't need any encouragement from her. Why had I said it? I guess I couldn't bear that they were talking about it. I was trying to shut them up – and to stop feeling guilty. Shamila had told me Neeta tried to kill herself before. She had wanted to die. That should make it okay – but it didn't – how could it? It wasn't okay – but it wasn't my fault. I had to get a grip.

I sat twiddling my pen in history, flicking the pages of my textbook now and then to make out I was doing something. Mr Marshall looked over my shoulder at the two sentences I'd written but he didn't say a word. Sometimes having dyspraxia can be useful. Some teachers – like Mr Marshall, don't expect much.

What was Shamila doing right now? I pictured her sitting on a sofa, sobbing her heart out. In my mind, I was round there, knocking on the door and Shamila's opening it, saying, 'Oh, Michael – I'm so glad you came,' and we're sitting on her sofa, and she's moving up close so I can feel her all warm against me. Then

25

she's leaning into me, crying – and I'm putting my arm round her, comforting her.

Nick suddenly elbowed me. 'Aren't you going to write down the homework?'

It was the end of the lesson. Where had the time gone?

I had French after break, then lunch – and then, after that, everything changed. I was on my way to my form room when Liam caught me up, looking excited.

'Have you heard?' he said. 'Shamila's cousin – it wasn't suicide – it was murder!'

I froze. 'How d'you know?'

'Mr Marshall was talking to Mrs Deakin about it outside the staffroom. I heard them – they were talking about what they should tell us.'

'Hurry up, you two!' Mrs Deakin called to us.

We followed her into the room. My legs felt like jelly. I nearly went flying over Sean's bag. Lucky miss.

'Quiet now,' said Mrs Deakin. 'I have something important to tell you.'

She paused and took a deep breath. The room was silent. 'There's no easy way tell you this – but the police have now announced that the death of Neeta Gupta – Shamila's cousin, was not suicide. The postmortem has shown that she was murdered.'

Gasps rose from around the class. I sank into my chair. Liam gave me an 'I told you so' look.

'Who done it, Miss?' he asked.

'They don't know who did it or why. But I know many of you live near the canal and I want you all to take extra care.'

The bell rang.

'Michael – will you stay behind for a moment.'

I felt a surge of panic. She knew something. She must do.

'There's a letter for you here,' she said. She held up a handwritten white envelope.

I didn't move.

'Take it then, Michael. It's not going to bite you!' She had that worried look again.

I took the letter. What could it be? Why had I got a letter and no one else?

'Go on then – off you go. You'll be late for science.'

I went a little way down the corridor and stopped. I had to know what was in the letter. I had to know. My fingers tingled as I tore at the paper.

I read it and instantly wanted to tear it into pieces. It was only from Miss Yashim, the Learning Support Teacher. When I started in Year Seven, I had extra lessons with her to work on my handwriting. They didn't help much – I think she gave up in the end. Now she was starting up a lunchtime club with Mr Bates, the P.E. teacher, for '*pupils who might benefit from fun, non-competitive activities to improve their co-ordination*'. There was going to be a meeting about it on Monday. Miss Yashim hoped I would go along.

She could hope all she liked. It sounded to me like extra P.E. – not my idea of fun at all.

'Michael!'

I looked up. There was no escape. It was Miss Yashim herself, full of smiles as usual. Didn't she realise someone had been murdered round here?

'You got the letter then?' she said, seeing it in my hand. 'It's ideal for you, Michael. You will go to the meeting, won't you?'

I shrugged. 'I'll think about it, Miss.'

'Talk it over with your parents,' she suggested. 'You'd better hurry now – you'll be late for your next lesson.'

I nodded, though I had no intention of mentioning it at home. The last thing I wanted was Mum on my back about it.

By the time I got home, I'd forgotten about the letter completely. But Mum was on my back about it, almost before I was in the house – and I hadn't said a word.

'Miss Yashim says it'll be ideal for you,' said Mum, cheerfully.

Of course, I'd completely forgotten about her phoning the school. She'd had a go about Miss Fowler and they'd fobbed her off with the new group Miss Yashim was starting up and how much it was going to help me. Mum was full of it – wouldn't shut up.

'I want to watch the news,' I told her. 'That woman who was murdered – her cousin's in my class.'

That changed the subject all right. Mum started on about what a tragedy it was and how she always thought this was a safe area to live. I slipped into the lounge and put the telly on.

It wasn't time for the local news yet but I kept watching anyway. When it finally came on there was so much other news I thought they weren't going to show it. I guess enough people get murdered, they don't all make the news.

Then suddenly – it was on. A picture appeared of the woman and it was still a shock. There she was – young, Asian, with long, dark hair and a shy smile, staring out at me from the screen. I think there'd been a tiny bit of me hoping, praying that it wasn't the same woman at all – that the woman I'd seen was not Neeta – and was alive and well somewhere. But it was her. I was sure it was her.

'Police are appealing for witnesses,' said the presenter.

I gulped. There'd be other witnesses – wouldn't there? I mean, someone else might have come along after I left – they might actually have seen the murder – and had a proper look at the man. The police were doing a good job so far. They'd worked out quickly enough that it was murder and not suicide. Surely it'd be no time before they had that man in custody.

Chapter 6

I had to wait a week before there was any news. I came down to breakfast and Dad was munching on some toast.

'They've – *munch* – arrested – *munch* – a man for that murder,' he said. 'I just heard it on the radio.'

'That's a relief,' said Mum, coming into the kitchen. 'It gave me the creeps thinking a murderer might be lurking somewhere round here.'

If it was a relief to Mum, it was a humungous relief to me. They'd got him! I was off the hook. The police had sorted it and I'd been right all along not to get involved.

Shamila would be relieved too, I thought as I left the house. She'd been back at school two days, looking a right misery. I'd tried to talk to her, cheer her up, but she hadn't wanted to know. Her mates had kept herding her off like a lost sheep.

And now they'd got him – they'd caught the man! Of course, it couldn't bring Neeta back, but it was the next best thing. My luck was definitely changing. I was even surer of this when I spotted Shamila ahead of me going through the school gate, and she was on her own!

'Shamila!' I yelled. 'Good news, isn't it?'

She turned as I caught her up. I expected a warm smile, or maybe a sad smile – a friendly nod, or something. But her face was thorny, eyes sunken, angry, despairing.

It didn't make sense. And then I realised – of course! There could only be one explanation. She didn't know, she hadn't heard – and I, Michael Emmerson was to be the one to break the good news.

'Move it, will you?' came a voice from behind. We were blocking the path into school. Shamila turned to go inside. I followed.

'Shamila, please! Come over here, where we can talk.'

To my relief she came with me, to a nearby dead-end bit of corridor where we wouldn't be trampled.

I held my head high, ready for my big announcement. 'It was on the news this morning,' I told her. 'The police – they've caught the murderer!'

'*Caught the murderer.*' She repeated the words in a murmur, her lips barely moving, her eyes shutting and then opening again, expression unchanged.

'I . . . I . . . thought you'd be pleased . . .' I stuttered.

'Is that what they said on the news?' Shamila suddenly demanded, her eyes looking deep into mine. 'Did they say the murderer had been caught?'

'I didn't actually hear it myself,' I admitted. 'But my dad did – he said they'd arrested a man. I'm sure he wasn't lying about it.'

'They *have* arrested a man,' Shamila said, lowering her eyes.

'There you are then.' I frowned, utterly confused. 'Am I missing something? Why aren't you pleased?'

'The man,' she began in a whisper. 'The man they've arrested – it's my dad.'

'*What?*'

She didn't wait for my reaction but walked quickly out along the corridor.

'Shamila! Wait!'

31

She stopped suddenly. 'You won't tell anyone, will you, Michael? Please? I didn't mean to tell you – it just came out.'

'Of course I won't – I promise.'

The corridor was empty now. 'Come on, we'll be late,' said Shamila.

Mrs Deakin hurried us into our seats. Shamila's friends huddled round her. I could hear her saying she couldn't tell them anything about the man who'd been arrested and she didn't want to talk about it. I felt a swell of warmth. She'd confided in me – *me*. I was the only one in class who knew her secret. Then I remembered, with a flood of guilt – Shamila only had a secret because of me. If I'd gone to the police, even the next day, when the body was found, then Shamila's dad wouldn't be a suspect. Shamila's dad was Asian and the man I saw was white – without a doubt.

'Michael Emmerson?'

I looked up, startled. It was Mrs Deakin – calling the register.

'Yes, Miss.'

'Sean Finch?' Mrs Deakin went on.

I went back to my thoughts. What to do? There was nothing for it. I'd have to go to the police after school. I'd have to tell them what I saw. But what if they didn't believe me? Especially if they found out I was in Shamila's class at school – they might think I'd made it up – to help her dad. It'd look dodgy enough that I hadn't come forward at the time.

And even if they did believe me, how could I ever face Shamila again? She'd have to know that if it wasn't for me – not only wouldn't they have arrested her dad, but Neeta might not even be dead. I couldn't bear Shamila knowing that.

Anyway, her dad didn't do it. So whatever the police were thinking, they wouldn't find any proof. They'd have to let him go, wouldn't they?

At lunchtime I was shivering out in the playground with Darren and Nick when Miss Yashim came running up.

I tried to hide behind Darren but it was no use. I knew her exercise class was starting today. I'd been off school the day of the meeting last week, with a stomach upset. And I hadn't made it up – honest. I was puking all over the place. Even Mum knew it was the real thing. Lucky or what? But now it looked like my luck had run out.

'Oh Michael, I'm so glad I found you,' said Miss Yashim. 'I'm sorry you missed the meeting but you are coming today, aren't you? I forgot to tell you, anyone coming to the class can go on first lunches – I've arranged it. See you soon, then.' She gave me a big smile and walked away.

'What's all that about?' Nick asked.

'Nothing. I'm not going.'

'Come off it – first lunches isn't nothing. What are you hanging about here for when you can go on first lunches?'

Reluctantly, I told them about the exercise class. I was expecting them to laugh.

'Can anyone come?' Darren asked eagerly.

'No – you have to be chosen. And I'm not going, anyway.'

'First lunches –' said Nick, 'and a chance to be inside all lunch hour instead of out here in this perishing cold – and you're *not going*?'

'Yeah,' said Darren. 'Are you mad or what? Are you sure I couldn't go in your place?'

Their reaction was a complete surprise. I hadn't thought about it like that. Suddenly it didn't sound so bad after all.

'I guess it won't do any harm to go – just this once.'

I went into first lunches and nearly turned round again. It was all very well having more choice of food but the choice of people to sit with was another matter. I looked around for Jamie. There was no sign of him – he was probably rehearsing. I wouldn't want to eat with him and his bunch of music nerds anyway. I looked at the queue, trying to make up my mind whether to stay or go. That was when I saw Shamila.

She was right at the end of the queue, looking round nervously.

I hurried over. 'Shamila! How come you're on first lunches?'

'Oh ... I've volunteered to help with some lunchtime class Miss Yashim's starting up. She talked me into it – said it would take my mind off everything else. Some chance – but I thought I'd give it a go.'

She suddenly met my eyes. 'Are you helping too?'

'No.' I felt my face going red. 'I ... I'm in the class.'

'Oh. At least I'll know someone then.' She gave me an awkward half-smile and then went all serious again. 'Michael, what I said this morning – you haven't told anyone – have you?'

'No, of course not. I promised, didn't I?'

We reached the counter and both stared wide-eyed at the choice.

She chose chicken and I went for pizza and chips. They always run out of pizza by third lunches. Shamila headed for an empty table. I hovered about for a moment, unsure if she meant me to follow. She looked round, waving her hand at me to join her.

'I wasn't looking forward to having lunch on my own,' she said. 'I nearly didn't come.'

My heart leapt. There we were – me and Shamila – sitting opposite each other, away from the prying eyes of our year group. Only Jed – who's not in any of our classes, so he didn't count, even though he must be coming to Miss Yashim's class.

There was so much I wanted to ask her – but I didn't want to break the magic spell. I wasn't sure if she'd want to talk about it.

'Your dad,' I began cautiously. 'Do you know why they arrested him?'

Shamila shrugged. 'It was our nosy neighbour. She told the police she saw Dad arguing with Neeta outside the house that morning – the day she went missing.'

'Arguing?'

'Dad was worried about her – he knew something was up and he was trying to get her to talk to him, that's all. But he can't prove it. And he doesn't have an alibi. The police said it happened between 4.30 and 5.30 pm – and he was in the car on his own – between appointments.'

Shamila looked like she was going to cry. 'I wish

there was something I could do,' she said. 'I feel so helpless.'

'Maybe there is,' I said, my mind whirring. 'If...if you can find out who did do it – then they'll have to let your dad go, won't they?'

'And how exactly am I supposed to do that?'

'I could help.'

'*Great.*' She raised her eyes to the ceiling in clear disbelief.

'There must be a way,' I said. 'Give me a chance to think.'

I thought hard – as hard as I've ever thought in my life. I had to come up with something – and soon.

Chapter 7

'We'd better go, we'll be late,' said Shamila.

I gobbled up the last of my chips, as she put her still half-full plate onto the clearing trolley.

When we arrived at the gym it turned out we were late. The people in the class were nearly all Year Sevens and Eights. Most of them had already been paired with volunteers, who were mainly sixth formers. Miss Yashim hurried over, smiling.

'I'm so glad you made it, Michael – and it looks like the numbers work out just right – that's if you don't mind working with Michael, Shamila? It's so good of you to come and help.'

I held my breath, waiting for Shamila to say, 'No, actually I'd rather not,' but she nodded.

Then I got that squirmy feeling like I had when we met in the dining hall. I wanted to be with Shamila but I wasn't sure if I wanted it like this – with me having to show off my clumsy body. What would she think? It was going to be a major humiliation.

Anyway, I had no choice – so I found myself dribbling a ball across the hall, throwing beanbags into a bucket and walking heel to toe along a line, while Shamila made notes on a prepared sheet. This was to work out my baseline for what I could do. Then I'd be set targets and try to improve.

At first I was worse than useless. Shamila watching

totally put me off. Knowing that her deep, dark eyes were fixed on me made it hard to think about what my feet were doing at the same time.

Miss Yashim must have noticed how hopeless I was because once I got into it and began to concentrate more, she came over, saying, 'That's better, Michael! You're making progress already. See what you can achieve with a bit of practice!'

The most fun was sitting on a skateboard and going up and down along a line, keeping straight all the way. I was also pleased to note that one or two people in the class were even worse than me. I actually began to enjoy it.

After a while we sat down for a rest. Shamila and I were both silent. I hoped she wasn't going to ask me if I'd had any ideas yet.

'I never realised things like this were so hard for you,' said Shamila.

'It's not my fault – I've got dyspraxia,' I told her.

'What's that? I've never heard of it.'

'Don't worry – I hadn't either until two years ago. I had to do all these tests – and when the doctor said it was dyspraxia he looked so serious and Mum and Dad looked so upset – I thought maybe I was going to *die* of it. I nearly wet myself – I was that scared. But it's nothing like that – it's not an illness or anything. It's just a word for why I'm so unco-ordinated, and my hand-writing's so messy.'

Shamila looked puzzled.

'It's like this,' I explained. 'When my brain sends the messages to my arms and legs they don't get through properly. That's all. It's probably genetic. My mum and dad haven't got it but my nan probably has, and my uncle, only no one ever told them what it was called. I've got it much worse than them anyway.'

'That explains a lot,' said Shamila. 'I always wondered how come you sound so brainy when we have a discussion and then you hardly write anything down and what you do looks such a mess. I thought you were lazy and couldn't be bothered. Why don't you tell people about it so they'd understand?'

I sat there, gobsmacked. Had I really heard Shamila use the word brainy about me?

'Why, Michael?' Shamila repeated.

'Oh – I dunno. If they ask, I tell them. But it's not something I want to go on about, you know? And there's never the right moment to talk about it. I feel weird, bringing it up.'

'Well – I think this class is a great idea. And I haven't thought about Neeta for at least ten minutes. Are you ready to do some more?'

We carried on for another fifteen minutes and then it was time to finish. As we were leaving the hall, Shamila brought up the subject I was dreading.

'So – have you thought of anything then, had any brilliant ideas?'

She must have known I'd had no chance to think. But she'd used the word *brainy* about me, so I had to live up to it now. To my amazement an idea sprang into my head – just like that.

'How about...searching Neeta's room – to see if there are any clues?' I said.

Her face fell. 'The police have done that, you idiot.'

39

My face must have fallen too. I had gone from being *brainy* to being an *idiot* in less than half an hour.

'They must have searched every inch,' Shamila continued. 'They were there for hours. They even took away her laptop computer. You'll have to come up with something better than that.'

I wracked my brains all afternoon, desperate for an idea that would have Shamila smiling, and grateful and thinking I was *brainy* once again. By the end of the day I had come up with nothing. I hurried out of school, eager to avoid her. I didn't want to admit failure. Maybe if I had the whole weekend to think, I'd arrive at school brimming with ideas on Monday.

Shamila caught me up, running. 'Michael, wait!'

'Look, I haven't thought of anything, not yet,' I admitted. 'But I still think it's worth searching Neeta's room. There might be something the police have missed. It can't do any harm, can it?'

Shamila shrugged doubtfully. 'I suppose.'

Something in her face – the fear, the helplessness, made my heart thump so loud, I thought she might hear.

'I'll come with you if you want – help you look,' I offered. I knew I had the time. Mum and Dad were both working and Jamie would be at rehearsals. But I didn't think she'd say yes.

'Do you mean that?' she said.

'I wouldn't say it if I didn't.'

Her shoulders sank back with relief. 'Thanks, Michael. This is so nice of you. No one will be in and Mum said I wasn't to walk home on my own. I didn't think I was bothered – but to be honest, when I came out of school just now I felt scared – really scared. What if the man who got Neeta – has it in for my family – and is waiting somewhere, for me? I'll feel so much better if you're there.'

I gave her what I hoped was a casual 'no worries' kind of smile.

Chapter 8

As we got nearer to Shamila's road, I stopped kidding myself. I wanted so badly to help Shamila – but... hunting through a dead girl's stuff? I began to feel twitchy. It didn't feel right. I didn't want to do it. Why had I ever suggested it?

'Maybe this isn't such a good idea,' I said. 'Maybe it'd be better if I walk you home and then you do the searching. Or you could get Kelly or Leanne to come over. Anyway, you're probably right – the police will have done a thorough search.'

'But you said...' Shamila protested. 'And I wouldn't want Kelly or Leanne nosing through Neeta's stuff. They're driving me mad for every detail of what's happening as it is. You can't duck out now.'

'All right. You're sure no one will be in?'

'Of course I'm sure. If my mum found me on my own in the house with a boy, she'd go mad – mega-mad. I wouldn't let you come if I wasn't sure she'd be out.'

Knowing that didn't make me feel much better.

I could see her hand was shaking as she pushed the key in the door. I followed her up the soft-carpeted stairs and through a door into a small bedroom. She took off her coat and put it carefully on the bed. Nervously, I did the same.

The room looked more like a guest room than a room someone had been living in. In five months Neeta hadn't made much of an impression on it. There were no posters on the pale peach walls. There were books on the shelves – psychology textbooks, mainly, and a desk with a printer and a space where the computer must have been.

'We'd better get a move on,' said Shamila. 'You start there and I'll start over here.'

Shamila pulled open the top desk drawer and began to root around. I wished I hadn't stood so near to the bedside drawers. I'd much rather have done the desk.

Shamila looked up. 'Go on then.'

I pulled open the top drawer. It was very full. Make up, tubes of creams, cotton wool, tampax. This was dead embarrassing. I shouldn't be going through this stuff. I yanked at a box that was stuck. There was hardly time to read the word panty liners on the side as the contents flew out onto the floor. I hurriedly gathered them up. Panty liners – what are they for? Why do girls need them? This wasn't the time to ask.

'I can't do this,' I told Shamila. 'It doesn't feel right – these are girls' things.'

'It was your idea!' Shamila spoke sharply – reminding me that this was no game, no messing about – like I needed reminding. I shoved the box of panty liners back in the drawer and pushed it closed. Maybe I'd have better luck with the next drawer down.

I opened it. Knickers and socks. Great. It was then that I heard what sounded like a door slamming downstairs. It must've been next door or something. I looked to Shamila for reassurance.

She stood frozen to the spot.

I felt my eyebrows rising skyward. 'It's not...' I whispered. 'It's not your mum...?'

'It must be. She's coming upstairs! Quick – get in there!'

I stared in disbelief as she opened the wardrobe door and shoved my bag and coat inside, indicating for me to follow them.

'You must be jo—' I began, but her eyes were so terrified, insisting that there was no option, no time to argue.

'I'll get you out as soon as I can,' she whispered, as I clambered in. The wardrobe door clicked shut.

I swore silently to myself. And then again. About ten times. There was hardly room to breathe. It was pitch dark – only a tiny chink of light around the door. I was having to crouch so as not to bang my head on hangers. The floor of the wardrobe was full of shoes so I wasn't very well balanced. The clothes were pressed up against me on both sides, brushing my cheeks. Dead girl's clothes. I shuddered. Don't think about it. How long was I going to be stuck in here?

I kept as still as I could for a few seconds – listening. I couldn't hear a sound. I felt fidgety. I began gingerly feeling around with my hands. This was a jacket – it was padded. I identified a sleeve, and then a pocket – slid my fingers inside. A tissue. Nothing else. I felt for the other sleeve and found the other pocket. Nothing.

My hands continued exploring. The other side of me was a pair of jeans. Again, I felt for the pockets. Nothing in the back pockets. But something deep in the corner of one of the front ones. Was it a sweet wrapper? It was paper all right and it was small and scrunched. Not the

right texture for a sweet wrapper. More like a receipt –
or maybe a bus ticket. I held onto it, slipping it into my
trouser pocket as quietly as I could. It wasn't likely to be
important – but you never knew.

'Shamila!'

I froze.

Her mum was calling from the stairs – coming closer.
I couldn't tell if Shamila had left the room or was still
here with me. Did she have a plan? Did she know what
she was going to say and how she was going to get me
out of here?

Something tickled against my nose. I needed to
sneeze.

'Shamila! What on earth are you doing in here?'

The voice was so close I instinctively leant
backwards. There was a small sound as two hangers
touched – surely too tiny for her to have heard?

When Shamila spoke, her voice was soft and pained –
utterly convincing. 'I wanted to sit here, quietly, for a
little while,' she said.

Her voice was near. She must be sitting on Neeta's
bed – only centimetres away.

'I feel closer to Neeta here,' she continued. 'Oh,
Mum! Why did she have to die? I can't bear it! And
what's happened to Dad? How can they even think he
could be involved?'

Oh no. The sneeze I'd been holding back was coming.
I was trying so hard to stop it I felt like I was about to
explode. I buried my head in the padded jacked, hoping
to muffle the sound.

'Ahhhhh chooo!'

45

I had hardly finished sneezing when the wardrobe door was flung open. I tumbled out, bewildered by the sudden light, the hysterical shouting, screaming of Shamila's mum.

'Shamila! Shamila! What is the meaning of this – this *boy* in here?' she cried. 'Is it the stress – making me hallucinate?'

She pinched my arm – as if to check I was real. Shamila opened her mouth to speak but her mum didn't give her a chance.

'And don't tell me you didn't know he was there. I can see from your face – you knew. Your cousin is dead. Your father is in custody. And you are bringing a boy here – and in *Neeta's room*! Then hiding him in the wardrobe because your mother has come home when you don't expect her? That is it? Am I to believe my eyes? Am I? Never would I have thought it – *never*.'

'Calm down, Mum – please!' Shamila begged.

But her mum exploded once more. '*Calm down! Calm down!* You have a boy hidden in the wardrobe and you want me to calm down?'

'Let me explain!' said Shamila. 'Sit down and let me explain.'

'Sit down! Now you are ordering me about like a dog!'

She sat down, nevertheless, panting so hard she sounded like a dog and all.

'This is Michael,' said Shamila.

'Oh – introductions is it now?' said her mum. She gave me a scathing glance.

'He only came to help me,' Shamila continued. 'He walked me home and we thought if we searched Neeta's room we might find a clue – something that would prove Dad didn't do it.'

Shamila's mum wiped her brow. 'If what you say is true, then why, my girl, was he hiding in the wardrobe? You tell me that.'

'I was frightened that you wouldn't understand,' said Shamila. 'I thought you'd jump to the wrong conclusions – like you're doing now. I thought it would be better if you didn't know he was here. I didn't want to stress you, Mum.'

Shamila was crying now, sobbing.

'Didn't want to stress me? Didn't want to stress me?' her mum repeated.

'It's all true what she says,' I told her – finally finding a long enough pause for me to speak. 'I was only trying to help, honest I was. It was all my idea – please don't blame Shamila.'

'*Out!*' she screamed, as if she'd only just noticed I was still there. 'Get out now! – Go on – off with you. And never let me set eyes on you again! You keep away from my daughter – do you hear?'

'I'm sorry, Shamila,' I said softly.

She didn't look up.

'*Are you deaf!* I said *"Out, now!"*' her mum repeated.

I reached back into the wardrobe, grabbed my coat and bag, and with a brief glance back at Shamila, I ran down the stairs and out into the street, banging the front door closed behind me.

Why had I gone there? Why? Why had I ever suggested it? I couldn't bear to think what Shamila was going through now. I liked her – I mean *really* liked her.

47

I wanted to make things right. Only everything I did seemed to be wrong, making things worse for her.

If someone had been in when I got back home, maybe I'd have told them everything. I don't know. Maybe I wouldn't. I went upstairs to my room and sat on the bed. I felt exhausted. Thinking over what had happened, I suddenly remembered the scrunched bit of paper I'd found in the jeans pocket. I reached into my pocket for it. If only it was something important – then maybe Shamila would forgive me for the scene I'd caused. I unscrunched it carefully. It wasn't a sweet wrapper. It was a bus ticket. I sighed. Waste of time. But then, turning it over I noticed there was a number scribbled on the back in biro – it looked like a phone number. It was probably nothing – probably a friend had given her their number and she'd had nothing else to write it down on at the time. It might not be that, though – it could be the murderer's number for all I knew. I'd show it to Shamila on Monday.

Later that evening we were sitting down to dinner when the phone rang.

I jumped up to answer it but Mum got there first. Shamila! Was it her? (I hadn't given her my number but I thought she might have looked it up – wanted to tell me she was okay.)

Mum held the phone out to me. My stomach lurched. It was her. It had to be.

'It's Liam,' said Mum.

I picked up the phone. 'Hi, Liam.'

'Some of us are meeting up tomorrow,' said Liam. 'At my place. D'you want to come?'

48

'What time?' I asked.

Mum interrupted. 'If you're making arrangements, don't forget it's Grandad's birthday on Sunday.'

I mouthed Saturday to Mum crossly and she nodded.

'Yeah – I'll come,' I told Liam.

I like Liam, but I'm not always so sure about the others he hangs out with. Anyway, it was good to have something lined up to do tomorrow. I had to stop thinking about Shamila and her dead cousin or I'd go mad.

Chapter 9

The next morning I was woken by Jamie's violin practice. Even weekends – there's no break from it. I lunged, bleary-eyed, towards the bathroom.

'Hey, Michael,' called Jamie, 'do you want to hear the piece I've composed for Grandad's birthday?'

I grunted an obscenity and shut the bathroom door.

I was about to pee when the phone rang and Mum was calling me. No peace – anywhere.

I came out of the bathroom and she handed me the cordless phone. It was Liam.

'Change of plan,' he said. 'The others want to go swimming.'

'Count me out,' I said, disappointed.

'You can still come – splash about in the shallow end. No one will mind.'

I grimaced. 'No thanks.'

'Meet us after then,' said Liam. 'In the café by the pool.'

I hesitated. Anything would be better than hanging around here while Jamie perfected his piece for Grandad. 'All right. What time?'

'Say... half eleven?'

'See you there then.'

I took the bus to the leisure centre. As it jolted to a halt outside, I started to feel weird. It was a long time since I'd been anywhere near that pool. It's where they took us from primary school in Year Six. Swimming lessons. *Bad memories*. I'd tried hard enough but I couldn't get the hang of it. My arms and legs wouldn't do the right things. Everyone sniggering – that's what I remember most. I got in such a state – I refused to go to school on swimming days. In the end they let me off. Mum told them she'd get me private lessons. I told Mum I'd learn when I'm older.

I went up the steps and pushed the glass door. The heat and smell of chlorine hit me and I felt instantly queasy. I wished I hadn't come. I told myself not to be an idiot – I was only going to the café.

A voice in my ear made me jump. 'I don't believe it! Mickey Mouse at the swimming pool! Where's your armbands then?'

It was Sean Finch – with a smacking great grin on his face.

Now I *really* wanted to go home. But Sean and his lookalike younger brother Freddy were between me and the way out. I turned my back on them and headed quickly up the flight of stairs to the café. Sean was sniggering – sniggering like he had in Year Six.

The others weren't in the café yet. There were glass windows one side where you could look down on the pool below. I looked. It's a massive pool and there were a lot of people in it but I thought I could make out Liam and the others in the deep end. They had no fear. They swam like fish – as if they were born to do it. Why couldn't I be like that?

I bought a can of Coke and sat down and watched. After five minutes I started getting impatient. It was nearly quarter to twelve. I tried waving to attract their attention through the glass. They didn't see – but Sean Finch did. He and Freddy had just got into the pool. Sean gave me a wave and then started splashing about wildly. I knew what he was doing. It was an impression of me trying to swim in Year Six. He said something to Freddy, pointing up at me. They were both laughing. I looked away.

Freddy's in Year Seven, like Jamie. Everyone knows they're brothers – but people are always surprised about me and Jamie. It must be nice to have stuff in common with your brother – to be best mates and that.

I waited ten minutes more. Liam and the others were still in the pool. It was definitely them. I reckon they'd completely forgotten about meeting me. Great friends, they were. I'd had enough. I got up and left.

I pulled on my gloves, shivering at the chill outside, and walked miserably towards the bus stop. A man some distance ahead caught my eye. He had a black beanie hat and black jacket. His white neck stuck out in between. My heart leapt. It couldn't be . . . The clothes, the build, the shape of the head – everything about him was the same – the same as the man by the canal. I was seeing him from the same angle – and about the same distance. I'd never thought I'd recognise him – but I did. It was him. I knew it was.

He passed the bus stop and I followed. There was no time to think – I had to keep him in sight. I had to see where he went. But he mustn't know I was following him.

Luckily there were enough people around to give me cover but not so many that I might lose him. The road was straight too, which was an added bonus. We came to the shops. Then he turned off down a side turning. I followed, cautiously. It was quieter here, but there was no reason why he should suspect anything. I was doing fine. I felt a buzz of excitement. I'd never trailed anyone before. He turned off again, crossed the road and then turned down an even smaller street. I waited a few seconds to put some distance between us. But I mustn't let him get away.

I edged round the corner – and nearly jumped out of my skin. He was standing there – hands on hips – facing me. I should've turned and run but I kept staring at his face. I was seeing it for the first time – the face of a murderer. I couldn't move. He looked hard, mean – his eyes narrow and angry.

'What's your game, sonny?'

I breathed in sharply. The voice. This man had a clear Irish accent. It wasn't him. It wasn't him at all.

I felt a complete fool. I didn't know what to say.

'I'm... on my way to a friend's place,' I told him.

He smirked. 'Try again.'

I thought fast. The word 'game' hung in my head.

'It's... it's a game, that's all,' I told him. 'Me and my mates – we're seeing how long we can trail someone without them catching on. It's only bit of fun.'

The man raised his eyebrows. His face relaxed. He was still suspicious but I think he could see I was no threat. 'You're not much good at it then, are you?'

I shook my head, looking at the pavement.

'Go on, off with you,' he said. 'And find something better to do with your time.'

I turned back the way I'd come, kicking at an icy puddle with my foot. The ice cracked and the brown water underneath splashed up over my trainer, wetting my sock. I spat angrily at the puddle. At least I hadn't gone to the police about the fight. I'd make a totally useless witness. I could've identified the wrong man, got someone innocent sent down. I'd been right to keep quiet.

I walked to the end of the road and stopped. Which way had I come? I'd been so focused on the man, I hadn't noticed. I didn't have a clue where I was. I walked some way before I realised it was wrong. There was a postbox and a shop on the corner that I definitely hadn't passed.

There was nothing for it – I'd have to ask someone. I went into the shop. It was a newsagent's – and I was reassured by the warmth and chocolate bars all around. I picked one up.

'Can you tell me the way to the leisure centre?' I asked as I paid.

'Walk to the end of the road then turn right, turn left at the traffic lights and then left again and it's along on the right,' said the shop assistant.

I felt relieved, until I reached the end of the road. 'Turn right,' she'd said. But which way was right? Sometimes I get muddled about left and right and my sense of direction is not up to much. Mum says it's to do with my dyspraxia. I'm not sure how. It must be the same part of the brain that does handwriting and stuff, I suppose.

I looked both ways. I had a 50:50 chance. I tried one – and didn't come to any traffic lights – but I thought I saw a turning I recognised. I went down it – but didn't come out where I'd expected. I walked back but I couldn't even find the newsagent's. I was totally confused.

I began to panic. The sky was grey as the pavement and looked as solid – like it might come slamming down any moment and crush me flat. Instead, it began to sleet. The icy specks stung my face and crept down my neck. I kept walking. I was bound to come to somewhere I recognised eventually – wasn't I?

It took much longer than I thought. At last, I saw a bus stop. There were lots of people waiting. A bus must be due. I'd get on it – I didn't care where it was going. The bus came. By some fluke, it was heading for the station. It was the right direction. From the station, I could walk home in five minutes.

About forty minutes later, I dragged myself into the house, wiping the icy sleet out of my hair. There was a lovely smell – one of Mum's homemade soups. Just what I needed. I went into the kitchen. Jamie was clearing up the last of the lunch things.

'Did Mum save me any?' I asked.

He shrugged. 'You're in big trouble.'

I stared at him in surprise. My mind leapt. *The police – was it the police?*

I didn't have a chance to ask. Mum was coming down the stairs.

'Where on earth have you been?' she demanded.

'I went to the pool – to meet Liam and the gang after their swim,' I said. 'You knew where I was going.'

Her eyes narrowed. 'Don't tell me lies!'

'I'm not lying. It's the truth. What's the matter? What's going on?'

Mum glared at me, like she was waiting for me to admit to something.

'Liam phoned,' Jamie chipped in, hanging up the tea towel.

'He said you never turned up,' said Mum, her eyes challenging mine. 'He wondered where you'd got to.'

'That's a lie!' I protested. 'I was there. I waited ages but they didn't come out of the pool. I got fed up and came home.'

Mum pulled at her sleeve, showing me her watch. 'And it's taken you all this time to get home, has it?'

She had me there. I wasn't about to tell her about the man, about following him and getting lost, but I had to think of something.

'I got on the wrong bus,' I said quietly, eyes down. 'I didn't realise at first, and then I had to wait ages for another bus back – all right? And I'm fed up enough, without you bawling on at me when I've done nothing wrong.'

I looked up. Mum had a half-smile on her face. She believed me. I knew she would. 'That sounds more like it,' she said. 'Oh, Michael, I'm sorry I shouted. I was worried that's all. I don't like the thought of you lying to me.' She put her arm on my shoulder and pulled at my coat. 'You'd better get out of those wet things – you'll catch your death.'

Catch your death. The body of a woman floating in the canal flashed through my mind. I wrenched my arms out of my coat. Mum thought she could say sorry and everything would be okay. She was wrong. What exactly did she think I might've been doing, if I wasn't with Liam? I could hear her calling after me as I stormed upstairs to my room.

Chapter 10

That night I got to sleep quickly – I was exhausted. I woke though, at 3 am, from a horrific nightmare. It may not sound horrific to you, especially if you can swim – but it was to me.

I'm at the swimming pool, trying to swim. All around me people are laughing, sneering. There's Sean Finch and his brother Freddy. The man I followed – he's there too – and Miss Fowler. And loads of other people from school – standing round the pool, smirking, laughing as I attempt a few feeble strokes of doggy paddle.

I try to concentrate on swimming, forget about the people watching – but the laughter gets louder and louder – so loud that my ears are ringing with it and it's echoing all round the pool. I want to get out. I have to get out now – right now. I reach for the steps but someone pulls me back. I struggle – but suddenly the water's deeper than I thought – my feet can't reach the bottom – and there's hands on the back of my head. I'm being pushed down – down – under the water. I can't breathe.

I'm frantic – struggling to push up and I can't. I'm going to die. I'm going to die. I struggle harder and then I realise I'm not in a pool – it must be the river – because the water is freezing and water weeds are tangling round my neck. I'm swallowing water and it tastes foul. Then suddenly my head breaks through the surface. I can feel the air – I gasp, I scream for someone to help me ...

'Michael! Michael – wake up!'

I opened my eyes, still gasping for breath, my lungs soaking in air as if I'd been starved of it.

Mum was standing by my bed, her hair all over her face, only her frown visible from under it.

My brow was wet with sweat. Mum found a tissue and wiped it.

'Are you all right? I could hear you shouting,' she said. 'It woke me with a start.'

'Bad dream, that's all,' I told her.

'What on earth were you dreaming about?'

'Nothing.'

'It had to be something for you to wake up screaming like that.'

'It's all blurry, I can't remember,' I told her. 'Something to do with swimming, drowning...that kind of stuff.'

Mum waved her hair away from her face. 'Would you like me to get you a drink?'

'No, it's okay. I'm fine now.'

'Are you sure?'

'Yeah.'

Chapter 11

Sunday was Grandad's birthday. A better chance to take my mind off everything. When we arrived, it was the same as ever. Slap on the back from Grandad and a wet kiss from Grandma. Hello to Mark and Jenny – my uncle and aunt, and my cousin Danielle in her super-tight jeans. She's nineteen and boring. Uncle Mark's all right sometimes – he's Dad's brother and like me, not musical. Well, he strums the guitar a bit and sings – but that's not counted as musical in my family. He reckons he has dyspraxia as well, though much milder than me and he's never done any tests or anything to find out.

Grandad tapped Jamie's violin case affectionately. 'So, what are you going to play for me today?'

Jamie started on a big explanation of his composition. I yawned.

'After lunch,' said Grandma. 'We'll hear it after lunch.'

Grandad didn't want to wait but to my relief, Grandma won the argument. 'You don't want a burnt birthday lunch, do you?'

Over lunch, Grandad started the conversation by talking to Jamie, as usual.

'How are you getting on?'

'What have you been playing?'

'How many hours do you spend practising?'

Jamie's responses were followed by numerous repetitions of: 'Isn't he marvellous? What a grandson!'

I knew the reason – but I felt narked all the same. Grandad had been a musical child. He wanted to be a professional musician but his parents thought music was for fun and not for a job. They said he should work in a bank – and he did, all his working life.

He was delighted that his son was musical and became a musician. To have a musical genius for a grandson was an even greater pride.

The thing is – it should have been me. When Mum got pregnant the first time, she and Dad thought it was a dead cert that the baby – me – would be musical. And, with a double dose of musical genes, I was bound to be even more talented than either of them. Makes sense, doesn't it?

Mum wanted me to have a head start, so while she was pregnant she played loads of classical music. She even put this kind of funnel on her stomach so that I could hear it better. And she was sure I was loving it, because every time she did it I would start kicking. It never occurred to her that I might've been kicking because I couldn't stand it. But she found out soon enough when I was born. She only had to pick up her viola or even a classical CD and I would start bawling my eyes out.

Dad thought maybe all that kicking in the womb meant I was going to be good at football. But he was wrong there too.

Then Mum got pregnant with Jamie. The weird thing was, he hardly kicked at all when she played music through that funnel. But he couldn't get enough of it when he was born. Of course, I can't remember him being born because I was only two. But I know he loved music right from the start because Mum doesn't stop going on about it. She could just put on Beethoven's Pastoral Symphony and baby Jamie would be in ecstasy for hours. So the happier Jamie was, the grouchier I'd get because I couldn't stand it. But I was grouchy most of the time, whether there was music on or not, so the music won. The music always wins.

'Fantastic, Jamie, fantastic!' said Grandad.

He'd finally finished with Jamie. Now it was my turn. 'And how are you doing, Michael?'

I shrugged. 'All right.'

'What are you up to these days?'

'Nothing much.'

He laughed. 'You have your own talents. One day you'll make your grandad proud – I'm sure of that.'

I wanted to ask, 'What talents?' That would have stumped him. But I kept quiet. It's not that I wish I was musical like Jamie. I'd like to be good at something, that's all.

Grandad turned to Danielle. 'And how's my university girl then?'

'It's brilliant. I love it,' said Danielle. 'Psychology is so interesting. I've decided I definitely want to have a career in it.'

'Have you made friends there?' asked Grandma.

'Yes – loads. And staying local means some of my school friends are there too. I was having a great time – only now Mum and Dad won't even let me go out on my own in the evenings...'

She paused to give a darting glare towards her dad.

'Why on earth not?' asked Grandma.

'You know, since that girl at my Uni – Neeta Gupta – went and got herself murdered.'

I was so shocked to hear the name, I gulped. The gulp wouldn't have mattered if I hadn't had a mouthful of chunky minestrone soup at the time. Some of it went down the wrong way. I spluttered – and before I could get my hand to my mouth, the rest came spurting out. I couldn't stop it.

'*Oh, Michael!*' I heard, as I stood up, coughing, choking, not knowing who said it – but aware enough to see that the white tablecloth, the cutlery, glasses, side plates – my pullover, Mum's arm, and even Gran's nose, were all splattered with orange specks.

Jamie was making 'yuck' noises; Grandad began whacking me on the back.

'Are you all right, Michael?'

'Is he all right?'

'Here, drink some water.'

'Don't worry, no harm done. I'll get a cloth,' I heard Gran say, as she went running into the kitchen.

I took the glass of water from Dad and staggered out into the hallway, still coughing. The fuss was unbearable. I wished I could disappear. I made for the loo and locked myself in.

I sat on the loo lid, sipping the water, the coughing gradually easing as the voices calling, 'Michael, Michael, are you all right in there?' came through the door.

Total humiliation. But I couldn't stay in there forever. A few moments after I'd heard the 'Leave him, leave him, he'll come out when he's ready,' I came out.

Dad shook his head at me with that 'you're a disgrace' look on his face. This was too much. I turned back towards the door.

'Don't worry, Michael, I know it was an accident,' said Gran. 'Come and eat your main course.'

I stood, dithering in the doorway. I wasn't exactly keen on spending the rest of the afternoon locked in the loo. And Gran's chicken supreme was very tempting. I was relieved to see that Gran had wiped the orange specks from her nose. The tablecloth had wet patches on it where orange specks had been sponged off and so did Mum's sleeve. The glasses had either been washed or replaced. Only the red blobs down my pullover were clear evidence of my crime.

'Michael,' Dad began.

'Leave him,' Mum interrupted. 'Sit down, Michael. Come on.'

I sat down and ate, sulkily.

I knew Dad was giving me dirty looks. There was silence for a while, then Gran restarted the conversation.

'Did you know her?' she asked Danielle.

'Know who?'

'The girl – Neeta whatever her name was – the one who was murdered.'

'Oh – her. No, not really. There's thousands of students. I did talk to her once – it was at a volunteer training session. She seemed nice. We both signed up to do voluntary work.'

'Didn't you say her cousin's in your class, Michael?' said Mum.

I nodded. I was not in the mood for talking.

'What voluntary work are you doing?' Grandma asked Danielle.

'I'm helping disabled kids with swimming. It's only an hour a week but I enjoy it and it'll look good on my CV – that's the main thing.'

'You could help Michael,' said Jamie.

'I'm not disabled,' I protested, unable to let that pass. 'And I'll learn to swim when I'm good and ready.'

'Of course you will,' said Grandma.

I sat in stony silence through the rest of the meal. Grandad hurried everyone through dessert and coffee. I'd turned the meal into a disaster. Grandad couldn't wait to hear Jamie play. This was the highlight of his birthday, as it had been every year since Jamie first performed for him aged four.

We all sat down in the lounge as Jamie set up the music stand.

I tried to exchange a bored look with Uncle Mark but he looked happy enough. The difference between him and me is that though he can't play, he doesn't mind listening to classical stuff. I guess it's his age. And he hasn't had to listen to Jamie practising.

Jamie lifted his bow. The room was silent. As he began, Grandad's eyes half closed and he smiled blissfully.

Jamie was good. Even I couldn't deny it.

Chapter 12

When I got to school on Monday, Shamila was waiting for me.

'Are you okay?' I asked nervously.

She gave me a hard stare – so hard it made me flinch, as if she'd slapped my face.

'You mean apart from being totally grounded,' she said, 'and having both my parents raving mad at me – and saying they'll never trust me again? Not to mention my cousin being murdered.'

'So,' I said, trying to pick out the one positive note in what she'd said, 'does that mean they've let your dad go?'

'Sssh – not so loud,' she whispered. 'They released him on bail. He has to go back in a month. They haven't charged him but he's still the main suspect.'

'I'm sorry,' I said. 'And I'm sorry I sneezed on Friday – you know, in the wardrobe, and I'm sorry I ever suggested searching Neeta's room.'

'Didn't exactly find anything useful, did we?' said Shamila, her voice still sarky.

'I did find something,' I said, reaching into the front pocket of my bag. I pulled the scrunched bit of paper out and unscrunched it. 'It was in her jeans pocket, in the wardrobe.'

'What is it?'

'A bus ticket,' I said.

'A bus ticket – great,' she said, taking it from me.

'Now we have evidence to prove that Neeta travelled to the university by bus – in case we didn't know already – which as it happens, Michael, we did.'

'Hang on, look – there's a number scribbled on the back. I think it's a phone number.'

'Let's see.' Shamila turned the ticket over, suddenly looking more interested.

'It's not a local number. Shall we ring it?' she asked. 'Or have you tried already?'

'No – I thought – wouldn't it be better for you to take it to the police – let them ring it. I mean – what if it's the murderer's number? It could be dangerous – you know, if he knew someone was on to him...'

Shamila shrugged and pulled out her mobile phone.

'What're you doing?' She couldn't be going to ring it – not after what I'd said.

'I'll put a block on so they can't get my number,' she said. 'I'll see who answers and say I've got the wrong number. Here, you read it out to me.'

'I don't think we should...'

'Go on,' she interrupted.

I read out the number. She tapped it out and swept her hair aside to hold the phone to her ear. There was a long pause. I held my breath.

'Hello,' she said. Then her brow furrowed. 'Oh, I'm sorry – I must have got the wrong number.'

She disconnected, looking puzzled.

'Well?' I demanded.

'It's the Brunswick Cancer Research Centre.'

'*Cancer research?*' It was my turn to look puzzled. 'Well, I don't reckon they murdered her – I mean, unless they wanted her body for their research – but then I guess they'd have kept it – not dumped it in the river.'

'Shut up, Michael – I'm trying to think.'

'Think what? It can't be anything to do with the murder, can it? She probably wanted some information for her course or something like that.'

The bell rang then for registration so we headed to our form room. Liam nudged me as I sat down.

'So, what happened to you on Saturday?'

'What do you mean, what happened to me? I was there – in the café – waiting for you for ages. You didn't come out of the pool. And thanks for dobbing me in with my mum – she was dead worried.'

'I'm sorry – we were having fun – we lost track of time in the pool,' said Liam. 'But we weren't that late – you should have waited. And I did try you on your mobile. It's not my fault it was switched off.'

'My mobile's not working,' I said.

'Well, get a new one then. And what's this with you and Shamila?'

'What d'you mean?'

'I keep seeing you with her – just the two of you, looking all intense-like.' He smirked. 'You're not going out with her, are you?'

He was looking at me like this was a complete impossibility.

'So what if I was?' I said.

'But you're not, are you? I mean *you* and *Shamila*? No offence, mate, but...'

'Look,' I interrupted, not wanting to hear what was coming next, 'I'm not going out with her, okay? She's been through a rough time – I'm only trying to – you know, help her out, that's all.'

Liam shook his head doubtfully. Not only couldn't he believe Shamila might possibly want to go out with me, he couldn't even imagine that she might turn to me for help.

Not that I blame him. A few weeks earlier, I'd never have thought it possible myself.

At lunchtime Shamila grabbed me in the corridor – and I mean, *grabbed*. She literally got hold of my jumper and pulled.

'Michael, I've worked it out!' she said excitedly. 'It all makes sense.'

'How?'

'Come over here, where we can talk.'

I followed her. 'Come on then, tell me.'

Shamila came right up close to me so that she was almost talking into my ear. Her words came out in a babble that I could hardly take in. 'The cancer research centre – I reckon Neeta must have found out she had cancer and she couldn't bear to tell us. She would have known how upset the family would be. That's why she was so depressed.'

'But hang on . . .' I interrupted. 'Someone doesn't go and murder you because you've got cancer.'

'Exactly!' she said. 'The police must have got it wrong. It has to be suicide. Neeta must have known she was going to die anyway. She probably couldn't face the thought of dying slowly and being a burden on the family. It makes sense, doesn't it?'

I wasn't sure what to say. 'Yeah – but having cancer doesn't necessarily mean you're going to die. Loads of people get better from it, don't they? Surely she could have had treatment, or something?'

'Don't you see? That must be why she phoned the Brunswick Cancer Research Centre – to find out if there was any hope. Maybe it had already spread too much, or was a kind that couldn't be treated. If only she could have talked to someone.'

'So – what are you going to do?' I asked.

'Mum's picking me up after school. I'll get her to take me straight to the police station. I'll explain – and I'll show them the phone number on the bus ticket. They'll have to stop accusing Dad once they know the truth.

'Thank you so much, Michael, for finding this. It looks like your idea worked after all. You found something the police must have missed – something to show Dad didn't do it.'

I stood there, dumbfounded. What should I do? What would you have done? She was so convinced she had worked it out. She could have convinced me too if I didn't know otherwise. She was so sure – I couldn't have changed her mind – not unless I'd told her truth – what I'd seen.

I don't know if you can understand but by then it felt impossible to say anything, even if I'd wanted to. It was as if I'd shut that bit of truth in a box in the back of my mind and lost the key. I knew it was in there – but I had no way of opening the box.

Chapter 13

The next day Shamila came to school looking as sullen as hell.

'What happened?' I asked, edgily. 'Did you talk to the police?'

Shamila looked down, kicking at the dust. 'They treated me like dirt,' she said. 'They didn't want to listen – it's like they've got it all worked out. They said they'd talked to Neeta's doctor. She was on tablets for depression but she didn't have cancer as far as they knew. The police thought I was making it up, to get Dad off. They were so patronising – like I was a kid who couldn't know anything.'

I listened, and couldn't help feeling relief. If I'd gone to the police – told them what I saw – it would have been the same for me. Why should they have believed what I said anymore than Shamila's theory? It would have been humiliating and a waste of time.

'Hard luck,' I said.

'They said it was definitely murder,' she continued. 'They can tell from the bruising on her body.'

Her eyes glistened with tears. The feeling of wanting to do something, something that would really help, came flooding back to me.

'Listen,' I said, thoughtfully, 'I was round at my grandparents on Sunday and my cousin was there – she's at the same Uni – where Neeta went. I could phone her, see if she knows anything useful.'

'Did she know Neeta?' Shamila asked.

'Erm – a bit, I think.'

Shamila shrugged. 'You can if you like.'

'I'll phone and ask her tonight,' I said. 'It can't do any harm, can it?'

'I didn't think your first idea could do any harm,' said Shamila, 'and look where that got me.'

'I'm sorry,' I told her. 'I really am.'

So that night I phoned Danielle. We don't normally phone each other or even talk to each other much. I wasn't sure how she would react.

'So – you decided to call me, then?' she said.

I was surprised but felt instantly relieved. She must have picked up on Mum saying I was at school with Neeta's cousin. She must have realised I'd want to talk to her – see if she knew anything.

'I didn't think you'd have the guts,' she continued.

I wasn't sure what she meant by that. The memory of the soup incident – my locking myself in the loo, came back to me. She must think I was a coward, not someone who'd get involved in solving a murder.

'Do you want to meet up on Saturday?' asked Danielle. 'And we'll see what we can do?'

'Yeah – that'd be good,' I said. I hadn't imagined she'd want to spend time actually meeting up but it would be better than talking on the phone. I'd have a real chance to pick her brains – explain how much I wanted to help Shamila.

'I'll meet you at the Uni pool, on Stratcombe Road. D'you know where it is? It's better there – not full of kids mucking about. Wait for me by the entrance. I'll have to show my student card to get you in as my guest.'

'B-b-b-but . . . ' I mumbled.

'You do want to learn to swim, don't you? I'm sure I could teach you in no time. It's all a matter of confidence. Ten o'clock be okay?'

'*What?* Errr . . . yeah, I guess.'

'See you then,' she said.

'Can I . . . can I ask you something?' I chipped in quickly, before she hung off.

'Will it wait until Saturday?' she asked. 'It's just that I've got an essay on Freud to finish for tomorrow.'

'Yeah – err, okay.'

She hung off.

I sat down by the phone. I remembered now. Last Sunday – at Gran and Grandad's. Danielle talking about teaching disabled kids to swim. Jamie saying '*you could teach Michael*'. It was all his fault for a change. Saturday night's nightmare flashed back through my mind. I swallowed hard. What had I done? Why had I agreed? Why hadn't I explained that I wasn't ringing about swimming?

It'd be okay though. I'd turn up at the pool and tell Danielle I was sorry but I'd got a cold. I'd say I'd better not go swimming, but maybe we could go to a café instead, because there was something important I needed her help with.

That'd work, wouldn't it?

On Friday at the exercise class I did much better at some of the exercises than the week before, especially skipping with a rope and throwing the beanbag in the bucket. Miss Yashim even asked Shamila if she was sure she'd written the scores down right last week. Shamila took it a bit personally. She looked daggers at Miss Yashim and afterwards she kept going on about it. I started to worry that she might stop coming to the class.

'Miss Yashim was only asking,' I told her. 'She wasn't doubting you. She was impressed with how well we've done, that's all.'

'Yeah, right. Like I can't count to ten. It was an insult – don't tell me it was anything else.'

She calmed down eventually and laughed when I asked her if she was still going to come next week.

'Of course I'll come – but for you, Michael, not for *her*.'

That was the highlight of my day!

When I got home I even remembered to start sniffing, in case anything got back to Mum after I met Danielle.

'Use a tissue, Michael – and stop sniffing like that,' Mum grumbled. Then she gave a sneaky kind of smile – the worrying kind – the 'I know something you don't think I know' kind of smile.

'What?' I demanded.

'A little birdy tells me you're going to have some swimming lessons,' she said, grinning.

'What *little birdy*?'

'Auntie Jenny.'

So Danielle had already blabbed to her mum and her mum had blabbed to mine. I should have known.

'I'm so pleased, Michael – but why didn't you tell us?' Mum went on. 'Was it going to be a surprise?'

'Yeah, but . . . I might not be able to do it this week – I think I'm going down with a cold. I thought I'd go along anyway and talk to her. I'm sure she can teach me some stuff without having to . . . go in the pool.'

'Nonsense, Michael! You can't learn to swim without getting wet. That sniffle doesn't sound like much to me. You don't want to waste Danielle's time.'

'I'll blame you when I go down with pneumonia then,' I threatened.

Mum laughed.

I had the dream again that night – the nightmare – struggling to swim, the laughter, being pushed under, drowning . . . If only I could have got on with it quietly – and hadn't had to start yelling and waking Mum.

She wiped my forehead with a tissue. 'Was it the same as before – about swimming?'

'Yeah.'

'Then it's a good thing you're going to have a lesson with Danielle today. Once you feel confident in the water, I'm sure these nightmares will stop.'

I hadn't told her the bit about being pushed under – but anyway, maybe she was right. I pictured myself swimming like a pro, with strong, fluent strokes.

'I wish I could just do it,' I told Mum, 'you know, like those baby turtles on TV. Each one breaks out of its shell, digs its way up to the surface and flips across the sand into the sea. No one teaches it, tells it the way. It gets lifted by a wave and off it goes. Little turtles do it. Baby ducks do it. How come us humans with our giant brains have to go to lessons?'

'I know it's not much fun learning but once you master it you'll never have to learn again,' said Mum. 'You'll wonder how it was you couldn't do it before and why you got so stressed out about it. And it won't be like school. It'll just be you and Danielle.'

'I'll give it a go,' I said.

Mum bent forward and kissed my forehead. I'm too old for that kind of thing – but even so, I didn't mind, just this once.

Swimming. I thought I would go through with it – until I got to the pool. The chlorine smell had me jittering, my stomach in knots. Danielle was there waiting.

There was a small foyer with a drinks machine and a couple of tables. 'Shall we have a drink first?' I suggested.

'Maybe after,' she said. 'I think it's better to get straight in and get started. The men's changing room is that way. I'll see you in a minute.'

I sniffed. 'I think I might be getting a cold,' I said feebly. 'How about you explain it to me this time – you know, how to swim, and then another time I can actually try it.'

'You're not scared, are you?' she said.

I gave up. 'No, of course not. But – we can have a chat after, can't we? Because there's something important I want to ask you.'

'Sounds intriguing. Okay then. Now let's get on with this swimming.'

So a few minutes later I found myself climbing down the steps into the shallow end of the pool. The water felt surprisingly warm, probably partly because I was so cold from the weather outside. But it was a relief, the warmth. I knew straight away that the water in my nightmare was cold – deathly cold, like the canal. Not like this.

Danielle looked stunning in her shimmering blue-green swimsuit. I felt weird with us both so undressed, so physically close.

'Have you got a boyfriend?' I asked her.

'Why, fancy me yourself, do you?' she said, grinning.

'No . . . no – it's just . . . you look lovely, that's all. I bet loads of men would like to go out with you.' I could feel myself blushing.

'Well, thank you, Michael. You're not bad yourself. Now how about some swimming?'

The pool was busy but not too busy and most people were swimming lengths. No one was taking any notice of us. It was okay – a bit like the exercise class. Once I got over my nerves I began to feel I was starting to get the hang of it. By the end I'd managed a few strokes by myself without feeling a complete idiot.

'You've done well,' said Danielle, as we climbed out.

'Thanks.'

Dried off and feeling fairly pleased with myself, I joined Danielle at a table in the foyer.

'What took you so long?' she asked, raising her eyebrows.

'Sorry.' I was embarrassed. I didn't explain to Danielle but it takes me longer than other people to get dressed. That was one of the things I hated about going swimming from school in Year Six. The coach would be waiting to go back to school and I'd be the last one ready. I still hate getting changed before and after P.E.

'So?' Danielle prompted, leaning forward. I thought she was still asking me about taking so long to get changed but she continued, 'What's this so important thing that you want to ask me?'

'Oh – it's about that girl, Neeta – the one who was murdered.'

Danielle looked surprised.

'Her cousin, Shamila,' I went on, 'she's in my class at school. She's completely gutted about it. I really like her – you know, *really*, and I'm trying to help her – see if we can find out anything that might help catch whoever did it. I know Neeta was at your Uni – I thought you might be able to help.'

Danielle smiled when I said *really* but she hesitated before replying. 'I can see why you want to help her,' she said. 'But surely it's better to let the police get on with it. I mean, it is their job. They've been all over the campus asking questions. I'm sure I can't tell you anything that the police don't already know.'

'Did you talk to them – the police, when they came to the Uni?' I asked.

'No.'

'Why not?'

She shrugged. 'I only met Neeta once. I had nothing useful to tell the police.'

I nodded. Danielle had met Neeta. But if she didn't think it was worth going to the police, then it was the same for me, right?

'You said you met her doing voluntary work or something?' I asked. 'Was she helping disabled kids too?'

'No, I'm not sure what she ended up doing. I only met her at the meeting where we signed up as volunteers. She was very serious – about helping people. She wanted to make a career out of it.'

'Do you know who she hung out with?'

'Yes – I can introduce you if you want – but I'm not sure if they'll take you seriously.'

'Please,' I begged. 'That'd be great.'

Chapter 14

'You can come with me now if you like,' said Danielle. 'I need to pick up a book from the library. We'll see who is around.'

'Thanks,' I said.

We walked to the main Uni building and I followed Danielle into the library. I was dead impressed – it was massive, and made our school library look like a bookshelf. There were tons of computers – and I mean *tons*.

Danielle headed for the psychology section, picked out a book and walked towards the counter. I followed.

'Are any of Neeta's friends in here?' I asked hopefully.

She looked around. 'Can't see anyone. Hang on... That girl there – I think I've seen her with Neeta. You wait here. I'll go and ask her.'

I watched Danielle walk towards a table where a dark-haired girl was bent over a pile of books, making notes. I saw the girl nod to Danielle and look over at me as she spoke to her. Danielle waved at me to come over.

'So you want to know about Neeta?' the girl asked. She looked me up and down, a little snootily, I thought.

'Yeah,' I mumbled.

'What do you want to know?'

'Anything,' I said, shrugging. 'You never know what might be a clue, you know, to who killed her – and why.'

She sniggered and then put her hand to her face to stop

herself. 'So you're investigating the crime, are you?'

'There's a girl he fancies,' Danielle chipped in, 'and it turns out Neeta was her cousin. He wants to impress her – you know how it is.'

Embarrassing or what? I squirmed. This was nothing but a joke to both of them. 'She's a friend, that's all,' I said gruffly, 'and I'm doing her a favour. She asked me to see what I could find out. So have you got anything to tell me or not?'

There was a noise behind me, someone clearing their throat. I turned sharply to see a snooty-looking librarian, with glasses too small for her face.

'Can you keep the noise down please? If you want to chat this is not the place.' She turned to me. 'And aren't you rather young to be a student here?'

'Sorry,' said Danielle. She gave me a look.

I knew it had been my fault – talking too loud again. What if this girl did know something? Was I going to lose my chance to talk to her?

'I didn't know her very well, you know,' said the girl, quietly, once the librarian had moved away. 'And she wasn't one for talking much. Seemed like a lot was going on in her head but she never told us much about it.'

'How about her voluntary work,' said Danielle. 'Do you know what she was doing?'

I looked at Danielle angrily. This was supposed to be my interview.

'She helped out at an old people's home,' said the girl. 'It was the one on Oaktree Road. She said it wasn't what she'd wanted to do – you know, old people. But no one else had signed up to it so she felt "obliged" to. She was really enjoying it. There was one lady she'd got close to . . .' The girl screwed her eyes up in thought. 'Elsie – that was it, I'm sure.'

'Thanks,' I said eagerly. At last – a bit of information. Maybe Neeta had told Elsie something. At least I had something to tell Shamila.

The girl stood up. 'Look, I've got to go now.'

'Thanks,' I repeated.

'I went to the Uni,' I told Shamila on Monday, 'and I talked to a girl Neeta used to hang out with sometimes.'

Shamila looked dead impressed. 'You did that for me, Michael?' Her voice was soft and grateful.

'It wasn't for anyone else, was it?' I said, smiling.

This wasn't strictly true, of course. It was for me I was doing it as much as for her – but that was my guilty secret – something she would never know.

'What did she tell you?' Shamila asked eagerly.

'Did you know Neeta was doing voluntary work at an old people's home?' I asked. I was suddenly worried. I'd built up her hopes and maybe she knew it all already. From her face, I saw straight away that she did.

'Yes,' she said. 'What of it?'

'Did she tell you about Elsie – an old woman she got close to there?'

'Elsie?' Shamila screwed up her nose. 'No, I don't remember her mentioning anyone in particular.'

I smiled with relief. 'The girl at the Uni told me Neeta was close to this Elsie. So I reckon Neeta might have told her something, when they were chatting. Also, it

82

could've been Elsie or one of the other people there who had cancer and that's why Neeta phoned that cancer research place. I thought maybe you could go there and talk to Elsie – see if she can help.'

'Great idea, Michael,' she said, but her tone was sarcastic, not what I wanted. 'But, number one,' she continued, 'I'm sure the police know about the old people's home. They'll probably have talked to everyone there already. And number two, in case you've forgotten, I'm grounded.'

She grimaced.

'Anyway,' she said, reaching into her bag, 'I found something myself, something that might be important.'

'Did you search her room then?' I asked in surprise.

'No – this was in my room. Neeta lent me a pretty evening bag for Leanne's New Year's Eve party. Afterwards I must have put it away with my stuff by mistake. She didn't ask for it back and I'd completely forgotten I had it. I only found it yesterday when I was looking for something else. I found this in the pocket.'

Shamila held out a photo of a shy-looking little girl – skinny and pale with big blue eyes and long fair hair. She looked about six or seven years old. She was sitting on a swing in a playground. It must've been summer as she was wearing a T-shirt and shorts.

'Who's she?' I asked.

'That's just it,' said Shamila. 'I don't know. Neither do Mum or Dad – or Neeta's parents. I showed them.'

'It can't be important though, can it?' I said. 'This kid can't have killed Neeta, can she?'

'So you think Elsie killed her, do you?' said Shamila. She was clearly upset.

'No, of course not. What are you going to do with the photo? Will you take it to the police?'

'No. If you don't take me seriously then why are the police going to? Especially after last time – the way they treated me. I'm not going through that again. No, I want to find out who this girl is. If I get some evidence that this photo might be important, then I'll go to the police.'

I had a sudden brainwave. 'Maybe she's Elsie's grand-daughter, or great-granddaughter even? Maybe Elsie gave Neeta the photo.'

'Maybe,' said Shamila, but she didn't look convinced. 'Look,' she said, 'if you think this Elsie's so important why don't you go and talk to her? You can take the photo and see if she recognises this little girl. I'd go but as you know, I'm grounded. I can't.'

With effort I pushed away the sudden feeling of dread. I hadn't imagined going there myself and certainly not on my own. Once again I found myself wondering why I'd ever suggested it. Great clues we'd found so far: a cancer research centre, an old woman and a photo of a little girl. None of these things looked even halfway likely to lead us to Neeta's murderer.

But I'd have to go to the old people's home. I couldn't chicken out now. And maybe Elsie would know something.

'I'll go after school tonight,' I told her.

I reckoned I might as well get it out of the way – but how was I going to get in there? The staff wouldn't let a 'kid' like me start asking old folk questions about a murder, would they?

Chapter 15

At 4 o'clock that afternoon I was standing outside 'Springview', the old people's home. It was on the main road so at least it was easy to find. Now all I had to do was get inside.

I rang the bell.

The woman who opened the door had a warm smile and I relaxed a little. A smell that was a mixture of urine and disinfectant wafted over me.

'I've come to visit Elsie,' I said. She seemed to be waiting for me to say something else so I took a risk and added, 'She's my great-aunt.'

'Oh – that's nice. I'm sure she'll be pleased to see you.'

The woman led me into a hallway and then she turned into what looked like a kitchen. I wasn't sure whether I was meant to follow but before I had decided she reappeared.

'Here, you can take Elsie her cup of tea. She asked for it a while ago but I've been rushed off my feet. It's my first week working here, you see.'

She handed me a very full cup on a saucer. 'She's through there in the lounge.'

I held the saucer and looked in horror at the tea that was already threatening to spill over, before I'd even taken a step.

'Isn't it a bit full for her to manage?' I said uneasily.

'No – she'll be fine,' said the woman who was already disappearing through another doorway.

I walked robotically towards the lounge, trying desperately to keep my hands steady and to keep my feet taking small steps one in front of the other. The lounge seemed a mile away. I had to stand aside for a man with a Zimmer frame to pass going the other way. I think he was moving faster than me.

The lounge had armchairs all round the sides. About eight people, mostly shrivelled-looking, were sitting, in various states of alertness.

How was I to know which one was Elsie? A bit more tea slurped into the saucer as I hesitated.

'Is that my tea?' a woman croaked from the corner. She looked rather fierce, with a narrow, wrinkled face and down-turned mouth.

'Yes, I think so ... that's ... if you're Elsie?'

To be honest, I was hoping she wasn't Elsie. She didn't look very friendly.

But she nodded and took the tea gratefully, in steadier hands than mine. Before I could warn her about the wet saucer she had lifted the cup to her mouth. Tea dripped onto her cardigan and she tut-tutted.

'Sorry, I spilt a bit,' I muttered with embarrassment. 'Do you know where I can find a cloth – or a tissue?'

She pointed to a shelf and I hurriedly fetched a tissue. She wiped her cardigan and then the saucer and handed the wet tissue back to me.

'Is there a bin?' I asked, looking round.

She raised her eyebrows and pointed to the far corner.

I put the tissue in the bin and came back, hovering awkwardly in front of her.

After a few moments she looked up at me quizzically.

'I know I'm getting on – but still, you're a bit young to work here, aren't you?'

'I'm helping out,' I said. 'You know, voluntary work.'

'What a good boy,' she said, sounding as if she'd like to pinch my cheek any minute. It was lucky she had a cup of tea in her hands.

A sad, glassy look suddenly swept across her face. 'We did have someone helping out here before – you know, a volunteer,' she said, 'not as young as you. Lovely girl, she was. Tragic.'

'What happened?' I asked. I couldn't believe my luck that we'd reached the subject of Neeta so quickly.

She leaned forward and whispered, 'Murdered, she was. Nasty business.'

'You knew her well, then?' I asked.

'Such a lovely girl,' Elsie repeated dreamily. 'Great chats we used to have.'

'What kind of things did you talk about?' I asked.

She sat back, giving me a suspicious look. 'What's it to you? Questions, questions. We've had the police here and all sorts asking questions. That poor dear girl. Mind you, I had those coppers fooled.'

She leaned forward again collusively. 'Made out I was gaga, I did.'

'Why's that?' I asked.

'What did I want with their questions? Not going to bring her back, was it? My hubby, God rest his soul, he had a few run-ins with the police in his time. Petty stuff – you know, nothing bad. He'd never harm a fly, my Alf. He *retired* like, after a bit. It was after he'd done some time inside. When he came out he said never again. He went straight – straight as a nail, but did those coppers leave him alone? Like heck they did. Pestering us every other day with something or other.'

'But...did you know something?' I asked. 'Something you could have told the police, if you'd wanted to?'

'Know something? I don't know who murdered her, if that's what you mean.'

She sipped her tea noisily.

I wondered what else to say. 'Are you...feeling well?' I asked finally, changing tack.

She looked puzzled.

'I mean, your health, you know...how are you?'

'Feeling well? Considerate lad, aren't you? I can't complain, I suppose. My legs play me up, that's my main bother. That's why I had to come in here. Kept falling over.'

'I hope you don't mind me asking but you don't ...have cancer, do you?'

'*Cancer?*' Her head jerked up in alarm and I knew it had been a big mistake to ask.

'Cancer,' she repeated, gasping. 'No one's told me. Are you saying I've got cancer and no one's told me?'

'No, no,' I exclaimed. 'It's nothing like that. I'm sure I must have mixed you up with someone else.'

The woman who'd opened the door to me came in at that moment, flustered but cheerful. Luckily she was too flustered to notice the anxiety on Elsie's face.

'Who said you didn't have any family?' she called to Elsie. 'And here's your great-nephew come to visit. You're luckier than a lot of them.'

She pushed a stool towards me. 'Here, there's no need

to stand – perch your butt there. Elsie likes a good natter, don't you, Elsie?'

Before Elsie could reply the woman had turned away, and was helping a tiny frail man towards the toilet.

'Did she say you were my great-nephew?' Elsie asked, once the woman had gone. Her eyes were wide and bewildered.

'Yes ... but ... ' I began.

'Maybe I am losing my marbles,' she muttered, frowning. 'Maybe I wasn't pretending to those coppers. Maybe I'm gaga for real. I don't recognise you at all. I'd swear I've never set eyes on you in my life. Great-nephew? And what was it you said about cancer?'

I felt panic rising inside me. I was handling this all wrong. 'Don't worry, please. It's nothing to do with you,' I assured her. It was my turn to lean forward. 'I'm a friend of Neeta's cousin,' I said quietly. 'She's asked me to help her try to find out who killed Neeta, and why. I'm only pretending to be your great-nephew.'

'Phew – that's a relief,' she said. 'But I don't think I can help you there. As I said before, I've no idea who did it.'

I reached into my pocket for the photo. 'I wondered if you might recognise this child?' I asked, holding it out to her. She handed me her empty cup and saucer and took the photo.

Holding it close to her eyes she peered into it. 'Sweet little thing. Who is she?'

'I hoped you might know,' I said.

'Not a clue. Why? Should I know her?'

She looked worried again.

'No, it's a photo that was in Neeta's bag. I thought you might have given it to her.'

'Wasn't me, duck.' She peered at it again.

'Could it have been someone else who lives here?' I asked. 'Like a grandchild or great-grandchild or something?'

'I've not seen this little poppet come visiting here. You can pass the photo round if you like but I doubt you'll have much luck. Ethel over there – she's blind as a bat. And Freda and Joe...' She nodded towards two people opposite. 'You won't get a sensible word out of them.'

I looked around. The rest of the people looked asleep. It was useless. What a waste of time.

'I'd better go then,' I said, awkwardly.

She looked surprised and I felt a moment of guilt. 'Things to do, you know...'

I held my hand out for the photo but Elsie was peering at it intently. 'I don't know the girl,' she said, 'but isn't that the playground on Fairview Road?'

I perked up. 'Where?'

'Fairview Road – someone's idea of a joke that – the only view is those dingy flats and the old munitions factory. I can't be sure – but behind that swing...' She held the picture up, peering closer at it. 'Yes – it does look like those flats. They put that playground there to cheer the place up but it got vandalised in days. Covered in graffiti and all sorts. I used to walk past there every day on the way to the newsagent's. That was before I moved into a flat – and before I came here, of course. It had swings – and flats like that. I'm not definite mind. I can only say it looks like that playground to me.'

Elsie handed back the photo and sat back, yawning, her eyes half closed.

'Thanks – that's really helpful,' I told her. 'I'd better go now. I wondered – would you mind if I came to see you again? And would you mind not telling that woman, the one who works here, that I'm not your great-nephew?'

She opened her eyes and grinned. 'It's nice to have a visitor. I don't get many. But if you're going to be my great-nephew I'd better know your name.'

'Michael,' I said.

She smiled again and winked. 'Nice name, Michael. And good luck with the detective work.'

Chapter 16

Back at home, I thought over what Elsie had said. The playground on Fairview Road – it was something to tell Shamila – but I wanted more. There was little chance that knowing where the playground was would help us find the girl and we still didn't know if she was important. I churned it all over in my mind. If only I could think of something, something that would make it all come clear.

Shamila was waiting for me by the school gate the next morning.

'Did you go then?' she asked me.

'Yes, of course,' I said.

She smiled. 'Well?'

'Elsie hasn't got cancer and she doesn't recognise the girl in the photo,' I said, 'but she does think she recognises the playground.'

'Really? That's something then. Where is it?'

'Fairview Road – do you know it?'

'I can look it up on a map,' she said, her eyes brightening. 'We could go after school. Maybe she'll be there – this girl?'

'There's not much chance, is there?' I said doubtfully. 'Especially when it's this cold out. And if we leave after school it'll be nearly dark when we reach it. There won't be little kids playing out. Anyway, aren't you grounded?'

Her face fell. 'Don't remind me.'

'Do you want me to go?' I asked. I felt I had to say it, even though I thought it would be a waste of time – and map or no map I'd have a hell of a job to find it.

'It's not fair to expect you to do everything. I want to be involved,' she said.

'You could text your mum – tell her you've got an after school class or something,' I suggested.

'I could,' she said, looking more hopeful. 'What's the last lesson this afternoon?'

'PSE – we've both got it.'

She smiled. 'And Mrs Anson is off with flu so there'll only be a supply teacher. Feel like bunking off? Then we can get there for when the kids are coming out of school.'

'Really? Are you sure you want to?' I hadn't thought Shamila was the sort for that kind of thing.

'Chicken, are you?' she teased. Her face turned serious. 'I think finding out who murdered Neeta is more important than some rotten Personal and Social Education lesson, don't you?'

I nodded.

Shamila looked up the map in the school library at lunchtime, and we slipped out of the back gate before the last lesson. We took the bus to somewhere near the playground and walked from there. I was glad Shamila was with me. I'm sure I would have got thoroughly lost on my own.

'Look, there it is,' Shamila said, pointing.

This was the rough end of town. The playground and

the flats that surrounded it looked grim and un-welcoming. A burnt-out car sat, discarded, on the path. The walls were covered in graffiti and as we got nearer I saw that some of it was racist. I looked round at Shamila, hoping she hadn't noticed. She clearly had.

'We can go if you want,' I said. 'We don't have to do this.'

'We've got this far. We might as well wait and see the kids come out of school.'

We sat on the swings, which squeaked like stressed-out mice. There was no one around except a woman with a toddler who wanted to go on the little slide again and again. When the woman told the boy it was time to go, he started bawling.

Soon, some children began to drift through. Most of them were with parents and went straight through the playground as a shortcut to the flats the other side. A few stopped to play. None looked anything like the child in the photo.

'Shall we show it to them?' I said, pointing to a small group that was gathering by the climbing frame.

Shamila nodded. We walked across the playground.

The oldest of the children couldn't have been more than nine or ten but there was something intimidating about the group of them.

'What d'you want?' the tallest boy demanded as we approached. The rest turned to look at us with hostile eyes.

'Just wondered if you know this girl,' I said, holding out the photo.

'Give it 'ere,' said a dark-haired girl, shoving her way to the front.

'No, I wannit,' said another.

As they all tried to snatch it I thought it was going to get torn.

'You can all see it – just take it in turns,' I tried, without much response.

'Here – it's Amy!' said a smaller boy. 'Why've you got Amy's photo?'

'You know her then?' said Shamila.

'Yeah – I know 'er,' said the boy.

'And I do,' said the dark-haired girl.

'And me,' said another, not to be outdone.

'No you don't.'

'Yes I do!'

'What's it to you, anyway?' the taller boy asked us.

'Do you think she'll come here to play today?' I asked.

'Not today,' said the younger one. 'She i'n't well – she weren't at school.'

Shamila looked at me triumphantly. Maybe she was right – maybe the girl in the photo did have cancer.

'Anyway – I know where she lives,' boasted one of the girls. 'It's that house – the one at the end.'

'You shouldn't tell 'em that!' said the boy. 'We dunno what they're up to, do we?'

'Don't talk to strangers, that's what my mum says,' said the dark-haired girl.

'Why are you talking to *them*, then? You don't know them,' said the other girl.

The children suddenly looked wary – as if we might be about to abduct them.

'Don't worry, it's all right. We're going now,' I told them.

*

Shamila and I headed back towards the swings.

'Shall we knock on the door, then?' Shamila asked.

'What, now? I don't know. What will we say?'

'We have to do it,' said Shamila. 'I need to know why Neeta had this photo.'

I let Shamila go in front. I could sense the group of children in the playground watching us curiously.

Shamila rang the doorbell. A blonde woman with lots of make-up came to the door.

'Yes?' she said, squinting at us. The sun was low in the sky and was right in her face.

I waited for Shamila to speak but she seemed to have lost her guts.

'My sister's in Amy's class,' I said, making this up off the top of my head. 'She wanted to know how Amy is.'

'It's only a cold,' said the woman, shading her eyes with her hand. 'She'll be back at school tomorrow. Who's your sister?'

'Err . . . Sarah,' I said.

'I'll tell Amy she was asking. 'Bye then.'

She closed the door.

'Why did you say Sarah?' said Shamila, as we walked away. 'If there's no Sarah in the class they'll get suspicious.'

'You were the one who was supposed to be doing the talking,' I protested. 'I said the first thing that came into my head. Anyway, it doesn't sound like Amy has cancer, does it?'

'Having a cold doesn't rule out her having cancer, but you're right. It doesn't seem likely. I still think she's important, though. There must be a reason why Neeta had that photo.'

'D'you think Amy's mum might have known Neeta?' I asked.

Shamila sighed. 'Maybe we should have been honest – asked her outright, showed her the photo.'

'We could go back . . . ' I said.

We had reached the bus stop. Shamila looked anxiously at her watch. 'Not today. If I don't get back to school by 4.45 I'll have a lot to answer for. Mum's coming then to pick me up from my "after school maths class". It's quarter past now.'

'You'll be okay as long as a bus comes in the next five minutes.'

To my relief as well as Shamila's, the bus came two minutes later.

When we got off near the school, we walked round the back way to the back entrance. It was 4.40 and Shamila didn't want her mum to see us together.

'You'd better go,' she said. 'I'll be okay. Mum's bound to be out the front already.'

It was dark and I didn't like to leave her on her own.

'Are you sure?'

'Yes – go on. I'll see you tomorrow.'

Chapter 17

'You're late,' said Mum, when I got home. 'Where've you been?'

'There was an after school class,' I explained, 'extra maths. I wasn't planning to go but then I thought I might as well.'

'You should have told me,' said Mum.

'I didn't think you'd be home yet.'

'Next time, at least text me. I like to know what you're up to.'

'My mobile's broken,' I reminded her. 'Mum, do you think I could have a new one for my birthday?'

'Only if you promise to look after it better than the last one,' she said.

'Yeah – I will.'

'So did you learn anything?' she asked.

'What d'you mean?'

'In this maths class. It wasn't that Miss Fowler taking it I presume?'

'No – it was another teacher. It was okay. I'd better get on with my homework. Is Jamie in?'

'No – he's rehearsing. Dad's picking him up on his way home.'

I went upstairs and tried to get on with my history homework. At least I could do it on the computer rather than write it. I'm slow at typing but the good thing is – teachers can actually read my work and it doesn't look a complete mess. I reckon I was born before my time. In a few years, no one will have to write anything – even at school everyone will have a laptop computer. Just my luck to be born too soon.

I'll never forget when I was in the reception class at infant school and we were learning to write our names. I sat next to a boy called Tom Hill and I was so jealous of him, I can't tell you. He had only seven letters – and most of them were easy ones. Michael Emmerson – I had fifteen – more than double – and it felt impossible. Once I even asked him if we could swap names. He was good at writing – he'd have had no problem with my name. But he looked at me like I was mad. I was the last child in the class to learn to write my name.

'Michael! Will you come and lay the table?' Mum called.

I ignored her.

'Michael! Did you hear me?'

'I'll be down in a minute,' I yelled.

'Now, Michael. It's nearly ready and your dad'll be back with Jamie any minute.'

I turned off the computer and slouched down the stairs.

It wasn't often that we all sat down to eat together. The conversation, as usual, drifted towards music and stayed there. I kept quiet. I had other things on my mind – like solving a murder.

'Can I have some extra pocket money this week?' Jamie asked. 'Mr Minton says I should get the CD of Ginette Neveu playing the Sibelius Violin Concerto. I'm sure it will help me if I have it.'

'Yes – I'd like to hear that recording anyway,' said Mum.

'Can I have extra pocket money too?' I asked.

'What for?' asked Dad.

'I don't know yet – but I don't see why Jamie should get more and not me.'

'If there's something you need, tell us, and we'll consider it,' said Mum.

'It's not fair,' I said. 'Just because I'm not into music.'

'Can I go now?' said Jamie. 'I need to practise while it's fresh in my mind – and I've got tons of homework as well.'

'Yes – go on then,' said Mum.

'I've got loads of homework too,' I said, standing up.

'All right – both of you,' said Mum, sighing. 'Go and get on with it. I suppose your dad and I will have to do the clearing up.'

The next morning Shamila wasn't in registration. I watched the door anxiously. 'Your girlfriend not turned up, then?' said Liam.

'She's not my girlfriend,' I muttered.

'Why not? You're spending enough time with her these days. Has she turned you down – or haven't you had the bottle to ask her out?'

'What?'

'On a date, you moron. Ask her to the cinema or something.'

'Her cousin's been murdered,' I protested. 'I don't think she's in the mood for the cinema right now.'

'It'd take her mind off it – you should ask her. It's probably just what she needs.'

'I don't think so.'

'Why? You want her to be your girlfriend, don't you?'

Liam was starting to get on my nerves. I was relieved when it was lesson time. But where was Shamila?

My first lesson was maths.

'Michael, where's your homework?' asked Miss Fowler.

I couldn't believe it – I'd slogged my guts out trying to do my history homework and forgotten all about the maths.

'I forgot it, Miss. I got confused. I'm sorry...'

'*Forgot it?* Is that the best you can do?'

'I'll do it tonight,' I said.

'No,' she said, thumping a book down on the desk. 'You'll do it at lunchtime – in detention.'

'But Miss...'

'No buts, Michael. And take that sulky look off your face.'

Detention. Miss Fowler was a pain in the neck.

Then, at break I was in the corridor, heading for the doors to outside, when I met Sean Finch walking the opposite way. I caught his eyes briefly and felt myself pull back. What was that look – that sneering half-smile? It made me flinch. Was it just the usual Sean – or was he up to something?

'All right there, Mickey?' he asked. I felt my skin crawl. I walked on, trying to dodge past him.

'It's rude not to answer when someone asks you a

101

question,' he said, blocking my path. 'You shouldn't forget your manners, not with me. And keep your eyes open, Mickey – there's danger all around – it's a dangerous world these days.'

He smirked and carried on past me. I felt hot and hurried for the doors – relieved to breathe the ice cold air outside. What had he meant – *danger*? Did he know something – something about Neeta?

Shamila – I felt panic surge through me. I had left her on her own in the dark to meet her mum. Today she wasn't in school. Was she okay? Had something happened? I nearly went after Sean – to ask him what he meant – but I saw Leanne and Kelly across the playground and ran over to them.

'Do you know why Shamila isn't at school?' I asked.

'Can't you bear it without her?' said Leanne, sniggering. 'Are you pining for her? Is your crush on her that bad?'

'Just tell me,' I barked. 'Has something happened? I need to know.'

'Ooh! Keep your hair on!' said Kelly. 'Actually she's just got here. She said she was going to the office to sign in. She'll probably be out in a sec.'

I went inside and headed for the office. There was no sign of her. I roamed the corridors. Then, I saw her. She was in the corner of the cloakroom. It was a dark corner – she was barely visible, yet I could tell, even from her shape, that something was wrong.

I went over. She was sitting on the bench, crying – sobbing quietly, her shoulders shaking. This time I knew better than to ask, 'Are you okay?'

She didn't seem to know I was there. I touched her shaking shoulder gently. 'Shamila – it's me, Michael. What's happened? It wasn't Sean, was it?' For a horrific moment I thought maybe Sean knew – knew what I'd seen – and had told Shamila.

'Sean? No – why?' she stuttered.

'Nothing – don't worry.'

She continued sobbing.

'I want to help,' I said softly, sitting down on the bench beside her, 'but I don't know what to say or do.'

'Thanks,' she whispered, sniffing.

'Thanks for what?' I asked, bewildered.

'For being here, Michael.'

'Do you want to talk?' I asked. 'Or I could get Kelly and Leanne if you like – or take you to Miss Wood – maybe you'd be better to go back home...'

Shamila breathed in sharply at the word 'home' then sniffed again.

'I don't know, Michael. I don't know what I want. It's like the world's gone dark – and nothing, nothing can make it light again.'

'I know it feels like that now,' I said gently, 'but it'll change, you'll see – things will look brighter. It's like now it's winter, isn't it? Winter seems to go on for ever. But it always gets to be spring in the end.'

I watched as tears slid down her cheeks.

'Not for Neeta – there'll be no spring for her.'

I closed my eyes and sighed. 'I'm sorry. I'm not helping, am I?'

'No – Michael, it's okay. I'm glad you're here. It was nice – what you said.'

I felt a sudden warm glow but her shoulders were shaking again.

'Let's go to the medical room – see Miss Wood. I think you'd better go home, don't you? It's no use being in school when you're feeling this rough.'

'No. Not home. You don't understand...'

'Has something happened?' I asked. 'Tell me.'

Shamila wiped her eyes with her sleeve.

'My aunt and uncle – Neeta's parents – they're still down here, right? I thought they'd go after the funeral but they've stayed. My Uncle Vikram is so angry – it's unbearable. He never wanted Neeta to come to Uni here anyway. He wanted her to stay living at home.'

'Why?' I asked, puzzled.

'She'd been depressed – he was worried she wouldn't cope but my aunt thought it would be good for her to have a fresh start. My aunt trusted my dad – he's her brother. She was sure Neeta would be safe with us.'

Shamila paused.

'So . . . ' I said, urging her on.

'I know they've got a lot of grief to deal with. I know they're bound to be angry. But it's not fair – the way they're blaming my parents. My uncle is saying terrible things.'

'Like what?'

Shamila shook her head. 'You don't want to hear.'

'I do – go on.'

She turned her head to face me, her eyes wet and shiny. She hesitated, then spoke quietly.

'Since the police arrested my dad – my Uncle Vikram, he seems convinced that Dad's guilty. Yesterday he accused him face to face – said he'd murdered Neeta. Can you believe it?'

I shook my head. This was awful.

'My dad was so furious,' Shamila continued, 'he couldn't control himself. To be accused like that – by his brother-in-law – it was too much. My mum tried to stop him but she couldn't. He punched my uncle in the face.'

'Punched him?'

'Yes – there was blood pouring everywhere – Uncle Vikram had to go to hospital. His nose was broken. I think they would have killed each other if my mum and my aunt hadn't managed to stop them.'

She sniffed, close to tears again. I tried to find words but I didn't know what to say.

'Now,' said Shamila, 'my uncle is even angrier. He insisted on telling the police. They're going to think my dad is a violent man but I've never seen him like that before, never. Do you see? Now the police are going to be even more certain that he did it. It's a complete nightmare. It's like two weeks ago I had a warm, happy family and now there's nothing but hate and misery.'

The warm glow I'd had, only moments ago, turned suddenly to a burning fire of guilt in my heart. It was so painful, I wished it would engulf me, annihilate me – like spontaneous combustion.

'It's a difficult time but you'll all get through it, 'I told her. 'Your dad didn't do it – so the police can't and won't prove that he did. Your uncle will calm down eventually when he realises the truth.'

'But what is the truth?' said Shamila. 'You can't be sure. I'm not even sure myself.'

'Sure of what?'

'That... that my dad didn't do it.'

I couldn't hide my shock. 'You don't honestly think he could have done it?'

'The way he attacked my uncle – maybe it was because what he said was true.'

'But your dad had no motive, did he?'

'Nor did anyone else.'

'Shamila – we'll find out who did it. We'll find out the truth – and it won't be your dad. Trust me.'

'We can't, Michael, we can't. I know you wanted to help and we tried, didn't we? It didn't get us anywhere. There's nothing you or I can do. Nothing.'

I squeezed her hand. It was cold – like ice.

'I'm so scared, Michael,' she sobbed. 'I'm so scared.'

'Me too,' I wanted to say, but of course, I kept quiet.

Chapter 18

Shamila didn't go home. She pulled herself together somehow and sat through geography with a glazed look in her eyes as if she was somewhere far away – much further away than Japan which we were learning about.

I struggled through geography and then had to go to lunchtime detention with Miss Fowler. I felt shaky and my writing in my maths book was worse than ever. How could I do equations? I couldn't think straight. All I could think about was Shamila. What she'd said that morning was getting to me. Her dad had dug an even deeper hole for himself by hitting her uncle and I might be the only one who could dig him out. There was no alternative. I had to go to the police. I couldn't be sure that they'd believe me or that it would help but I had to do it.

Once I'd made up my mind I felt calmer. But by the time the bell went for third sitting at lunch I had only done a quarter of the maths and I'd made a lot of mistakes. Miss Fowler was not happy but she couldn't stop me from going for lunch.

I didn't hang around to see Shamila after school. I couldn't face her. I took the bus into town and walked to the police station. I went up the steps, my heart pounding, and looked through the glass doors. A tall, stern-looking policeman was standing behind the reception desk. I remembered what Shamila had said – how they'd talked to her like she was dirt. I felt butterflies in my stomach, worse even than at the swimming pool. There was someone talking to the man at the desk, and two other people sitting waiting.

I went back down the steps. I had to think – work out exactly what I was going to say. Something like, 'I think I saw the man who killed Neeta Gupta but I only saw him from the back.'

I tried to imagine the policeman's reaction. I could picture him frowning and then laughing, asking me, 'And what use is that?' I'd say, 'He was white – I saw his neck.' Then the policeman would laugh even louder.

Maybe it wouldn't have been like that. Maybe he'd have taken me seriously, asked me into an interview room and taken my statement like I was an important witness. Maybe he wouldn't have had a go at me about not coming forward earlier. Maybe they'd have crossed Shamila's dad off the suspect list straight away. I'll never know, because I didn't go in.

I know you're thinking I was too chicken and you could be right. But it's not like I did nothing. Shamila had to be wrong about there being nothing we could do. I'd thought going to the police was my only option. Now, standing outside the police station, I started thinking again about the photo of the little girl. It might not be important but we didn't know that for sure. It had kept nagging at my mind since Shamila showed it to me. How and why did Neeta come to have that photo in her bag? If only I could find out. Wouldn't it be better if I could go to the police with something more than having seen someone's neck?

So I went to the playground. Don't ask me how I found it – luck, maybe. After three or four wrong turns, when I thought I was getting lost, there it was. When I saw it, I thought – I'm *meant* to be here – I must be. It was fate. But within seconds I began to feel edgy. There were no kids around at all. The playground was deserted, apart from a scraggy-looking dog, cocking its leg against the climbing frame. It was later than when I went there before with Shamila and although it wasn't quite dark, the greyer sky gave the place an even grimmer feel.

I looked cagily at the front door of Amy's house, wondering if I had the guts to knock, to tell Amy's mum the truth. When I say 'the truth', I don't mean the whole truth, just the bit about the photo being found in Neeta's bag.

I hesitated. I couldn't chicken out of this too – as well as the police station. No way. I tried to egg myself on but my feet didn't want to move.

Then two kids suddenly appeared in the playground. They startled me – I'd been so deep in thought I hadn't seen them coming. I think they must've come out of one of the flats the other side. I recognised the taller one as the girl with dark hair who'd been in the group we'd talked to before. The other girl was younger, with wispy fair hair. Could it...? I wasn't sure – but remembering the photo I thought it could, possibly, be Amy.

The dark-haired girl saw me and turned to the younger one, pointing back at me. I walked towards them, trying to emit an air of casual confidence.

'Hi,' I said. I shuffled awkwardly in the face of their suspicious stares.

'You's the one what came 'ere before, with that girl, in't you?' said the dark-haired girl.

She turned to the younger girl. 'I told you, Amy. He's got your photo.'

Amy stepped back, eyeing me nervously, her fingers twiddling her hair.

'Go on, show her,' said the dark-haired girl. 'Show her that photo. I told her you'd got it and she don't believe me.'

'Sorry, I haven't got it with me,' I said.

'Why've you come back then?' The girl clutched Amy's hand protectively. 'What d'you want?'

'Look, I'm not going to hurt you or anything,' I told Amy. 'It's just . . . I'm trying to solve a mystery. I want to know how a photo of you ended up in my friend's cousin's bag, that's all.'

Amy looked up at me, screwing up her face. 'Is you the one what told my mum your sister Sarah was in my class at school?' she asked shyly.

'Yes,' I admitted, 'but . . . '

'There ain't no Sarah in my class,' she interrupted, more confident now. 'My mum says you're a liar. Up to no good, that's what she said.'

'We shouldn't talk to him if he's "up to no good",' said the dark-haired girl. 'Come on, Amy, let's go.'

I moved to block their path. 'Please, wait . . . Can I ask you one question?'

'What?' said Amy. She was clearly curious and reluctant to be dragged away.

'Do you remember a photo of you, sitting on one of those swings? You were wearing shorts and a T-shirt.'

'You mean the one what was stuck on our fridge with a magnet?' said Amy.

I nodded eagerly. 'Yes – it might be that one.'

Finally, finally, it looked like I could be getting somewhere. 'What happened to it, Amy? What happened to that photo?'

'I dunno.' She shrugged. 'It disappeared. It were on the fridge for ages then one day it weren't. Mum reckoned it must've felled off and gone under the fridge. I tried to get it out with a ruler but there was only an old biro and lots of dust. It could've been there and the ruler didn't reach it – it was too dark to see.'

'When did it disappear?' I asked her. 'Can you remember? It might be important.'

'I don't get it,' said the dark-haired girl. 'You're a loony, you are. It was only a photo – what's the big deal over a silly photo?'

'Shut up, can't you?' I said angrily.

'It weren't silly,' said Amy. 'It were a nice one. Mum said I looked pretty.'

'When did it disappear?' I repeated.

She shrugged. 'I dunno.'

'Try to think,' I pleaded.

'If she says she don't know then she don't know,' said the dark-haired girl. 'Leave her be.'

'Are you sure you can't remember?' I asked more gently.

'It weren't today – or yesterday – or last week,' Amy said thoughtfully. 'It were before then.'

'Amy!'

We all turned towards the voice. A skinny girl, who

111

looked about eleven, was walking determinedly towards us.

'Amy! Mum says you gotta come in now.'

Her jaw was chomping vigorously on some gum. She looked me up and down and then turned to the dark-haired girl. 'This your new boyfriend, then, Natalie?' she said, smirking.

'No he ain't!' Natalie protested in horror. 'Anyway, Tanya – he's got a photo of your Amy. He keeps asking her questions and he won't stop even when she keeps on telling him she don't know.'

'Let me explain,' I interrupted.

'Go on then,' said Tanya. 'This better be good.' She gave me a toothy, gummy smile.

'Are you Amy's sister?' I asked her.

'Thought you were explaining, not asking questions,' she said, but I had seen Amy nodding.

'Do you remember a photo of Amy sitting on that swing? Amy says it used to be on your fridge.'

'So what if I do? What's it to you?' sneered Tanya.

'He's got it,' said Natalie, 'like I told you.'

'Will you shut up a minute,' I said crossly to Natalie.

'Yeah, Natalie, shut up,' said Tanya.

Natalie folded her arms angrily. 'You can't tell me to shut up. I'm going home.'

With that, she stormed off.

'So?' said Tanya.

'I'm trying to solve a mystery,' I told her.

'What *mystery*?'

'A photo of your sister Amy was found in my friend's cousin's bag. I'm trying to find out how it got there.

Maybe you or your mum knew, I mean knows, my friend's cousin. Do you recognise the name Neeta Gupta?'

This was a risk. She might have heard it on the news. I held my breath.

Chapter 19

'Nitagoop what? Never 'eard of 'er,' said Tanya, screwing up her nose. 'What does it matter to you anyway? So what if Amy's photo was in 'er bag? And if you want to know so much why don't you ask 'er – that Nitagoop what's-'er-name?'

'I can't ask her – she's – she's not around at the moment. It's a mystery,' I repeated, 'and I thought you might be able to help solve it.'

'What's in it for us?' asked Tanya, putting her hands on her hips.

'Well, errm . . . I'm sure I could sort out some sort of reward,' I said, 'that's if you can tell me anything that helps me solve the mystery. Amy says the photo of her on that swing was on your fridge and it disappeared. Do you know where it went or who could've taken it?'

'I know!' said Amy, suddenly. 'Maybe it were me dad.'

I looked at Tanya. She shook her head. 'Why'd he take it? He's got enough photos of us. What would he want with that one?'

'He could of,' said Amy.

'He ain't been round for ages,' said Tanya.

'He doesn't live with you then?' I asked.

'Na,' said Amy.

'What does he look like?' I asked.

'He's a bit fat and he's got long 'air – in a ponytail,' said Amy.

114

I was disappointed. I may have only seen the man by the canal from the back – but this definitely didn't sound like him.

'Anyone else you can think of?' I asked. 'Anyone who comes to your house, in your kitchen?'

'Mum's friend Trish – but she wouldn't of tooked it,' said Amy. 'And the plumber came, didn't he, Tanya – when there was that leak under the sink?'

Tanya shrugged. 'Dunno.'

'Who's the plumber?' I asked.

'I dunno his name,' said Amy. 'Think it's Rick or something like that. I can ask Mum if you want.'

'Yeah, but, Amy,' said Tanya, 'that plumber's not gonna of run off with your photo, is he, unless he's a pervert or something?'

'Anyone else?' I asked hurriedly. Bad thoughts were flashing through my mind. *Was* he a pervert? A paedophile even? And maybe Neeta had found out – and that's why he killed her. It didn't bear thinking about.

I bent down so I was eye to eye with Amy and spoke seriously. 'Listen – no one's been messing with you, have they?' I asked. 'You know, doing stuff they shouldn't to you?'

Amy stepped back in alarm. 'No they ain't! And if they did I'd scream and scream. Do you want to hear how I'd scream?'

She opened her mouth wide.

'No – no please!' I said. 'I believe you. I don't need to hear. Let's get back to that photo. Who else could have taken it?'

Tanya turned to me. 'Could've been one of Mum's

115

ex-boyfriends,' she said. 'But I don't think they'd want a photo of Amy.'

'Dan could of,' said Amy. 'He was nice he was.'

'But Mum split up with him yonks ago,' said Tanya. 'Your photo was still there after he'd gone – and he ain't been back, has he?'

'What about Craig?' said Amy.

How many boyfriends has your mum got?' I asked, jokily.

'There was Dan and then Craig,' said Amy. 'But she ain't seeing none of them no more. Done with men – that's what Mum said, didn't she, Tanya?'

'And what do Craig and Dan look like?' I tried.

Tanya shrugged. 'Just ordinary,' she said.

'Do you know where they live?'

'No.'

'Tanya, Amy – you get in here now!' We all turned our heads at once to see their mum standing outside their house, looking angry, arms folded.

I turned my face away, not wanting her to recognise me. 'I'd better go,' I told them.

'What about the reward?' said Tanya.

'Look – I'll give you my phone number,' I said, thinking fast, 'in case you think of anyone else.'

I scrabbled in my bag for a pen and in my haste half my books ended up tipped out on the ground. Hurriedly I shoved them back in, holding on only to my notepad. My writing was a scribble as I jotted down my name and the number. I tore it off and gave it to Tanya.

'You write like a three-year-old,' said Tanya, taking the paper and looking at it haughtily.

'You can read it, can't you?' I protested, embarrassed.

'Yeah, I can read it, *Michael* – just about,' said Tanya.

'Right, I'm off,' I said. Their mum was walking towards us. 'You'd better go in.'

I didn't look back as I hurried away.

Rick, Craig, Dan. Was I any further forward? As I headed for the bus stop, face down against the icy wind, I wasn't sure whether I felt pleased or disappointed. Somehow I'd been hoping to find the answer but I seemed to find only more questions. And maybe the photo had nothing to do with it at all. I could spend ages trying to track down Rick, Craig and Dan and it could all be a waste of time.

As the bus stop came into sight, I could see a bus pulling away. I ran but was too late; it had gone and I was in time only to see that it was the number 23 – my bus. I stood shivering, as the sky grew darker. A woman came and stood waiting too but she got on the 262 which came after about five minutes and I was alone again. I was growing to hate this place more and more.

A sudden loud shout broke through the noise of the traffic. It sounded like someone in pain. I turned towards the voice but couldn't see anything. Then there were more shouts – this time aggressive voices swearing, taunting. Then more yells of pain. What was going on?

Then I saw. Across the road, in the opening of an alleyway between two blocks of terraced houses, two men were laying into someone. The man was putting up a brave fight but it was two against one and a punch in the stomach had him reeling. He fell back, landing on

117

the ground. The other two men were kicking him as he squirmed, trying to get up.

I felt my stomach churn. The last thing I wanted was to be witness to another murder. I wished I'd never come back here, to this run-down estate. Mum would have had a blue fit if she'd known where I was. If I'd had a working mobile phone I'd have called the police. I would have – for definite this time. I thought about knocking on someone's door, telling them to call the police. There was no phone box anywhere near.

While I was hesitating a man drove past in a car, and, seeing the men kicking, slowed down, hooting the horn loudly. Did he know them – or was he trying to warn them off? Trying to warn them off, it seemed, and it worked. The two men scarpered down the other end of the alley. I hoped the car would stop and the person in it go and see if the man lying on the ground was all right. But the car carried on past.

I waited to see if the men would come back, or if the man on the ground would get up and walk away. Nothing. I willed my bus to come. I wanted to get on it – to get away from here. It didn't come.

Reluctantly, I crossed the road and walked towards the alley. The man lying on the ground looked like he was in his late twenties. He also looked a mess, his nose running with blood and his clothes trampled with shoe-prints. To my relief, I saw that he was still alive, trying to move.

'Do you need help?' I asked nervously. 'Shall I call an ambulance?'

'Piss off!' he said, hoarsely.

'But… you're hurt,' I said. 'I saw those men –

118

attacking you. Did you know them? Did they steal your stuff ... ?'

'Mind your own eff-ing business.'

Something in his voice, the way he spoke those words, made my heart miss a beat. That voice – it sounded so familiar. I was sure I recognised it. At least – I thought I did. Maybe any man has that vicious undertone when he's that angry.

He made a groaning sound as he managed, with difficulty, to pull himself up into a sitting position. He leant back against the wall, breathing heavily. Then he turned to look down the alley, as if wanting to make sure the men had definitely gone. This gave me a chance to study the back of his head – trying to remember.

No hat – but he had short hair. A long pinky-white neck. It could be him. But more than anything it was the voice, the grainy roughness, the intimidating drawl of it. My memory said yes. But my mind didn't want to believe it. It couldn't be, could it?

He turned back towards me. 'You still 'ere? Thought I told you to piss off?'

I was frozen to the spot now, and couldn't even speak.

'And no going to the cops, right? This is my business – I'll sort it out.'

With effort, he struggled to his feet, clutching his ribs and wincing with pain.

I unfroze and stepped back rapidly – afraid he was going to attack me. 'I'm going,' I said, 'I only came to see if you needed help, that's all.'

'Well I don't – so piss off.'

He took a few steps out of the alley, and limped back

119

towards the estate. Warily, I looked the other way, across the road towards the bus stop. A bus was coming. It was a 23 – my bus. Hesitating only a moment, I ran back across the road, car horns blaring at me as I dodged the traffic. I clambered breathlessly onto the bus, glancing back every few seconds towards the man. I wanted to get away – but maybe I shouldn't – maybe I should follow him.

The bus hissed and started off before I could change my mind. Anyway, it would have been dead hard to follow him, when he was going so slowly and with so few people around. If I'd tried to follow he'd have seen me, for sure. My heart was racing. If I was right, I had just seen Neeta's murderer being beaten up. Why were those men having a go at him? Did they know? I wished I'd been able to find out his name, find out whether he was Rick, Craig, Dan – or someone else. Then I would have been getting somewhere. Instead I was helplessly watching him walk away.

The bus jolted. I looked at my watch. It was a quarter to five. If Mum was home she'd go mad again as I hadn't told her where I was going.

When I finally reached my stop and stepped off the bus it was beginning to snow.

The phone was ringing as I went into the house. No one was home. That was something. I ran to pick it up.

'Hello,' I said, a little breathlessly.

Whoever was on the other end sounded breathless too. I could hear the heavy breathing but no one spoke.

'Hello?' I repeated. Was it Tanya – was she playing games? Maybe giving her my phone number had been a bad idea. The heavy breathing reminded me of the

120

injured man. But he didn't know who I was anymore than I knew who he was. And he certainly didn't know my phone number.

'Hello?' I tried once more.

Still just breathing. There was something scary, deliberate about it – or was that my imagination? Maybe it was a bad line.

'Hello, who is this?' I said.

The phone went dead.

Chapter 20

Still feeling shaky, I made myself a mug of hot chocolate. Then I went into the lounge and put the telly on. I hugged the warm mug for comfort, wondering if there was something else I could have done about the man. Maybe if I'd gone back to the police station, told them about him, that I thought he was Neeta's murderer – they might have gone after him, caught him up. But what evidence was there? I thought I'd phone Danielle – see if she could ask around at the Uni, find out whether Neeta had ever mentioned a Rick, Craig or Dan to anyone. At least I'd be doing something.

I finished my drink and picked up the phone.

My Auntie Jenny answered.

'Oh Michael, nice to hear from you! How are the swimming lessons going?'

'Yeah – okay, I guess. Danielle's a good teacher.'

'How's your mum and dad? And Jamie, of course?'

I had to give her the run down on the family's health before I could get her to put me on to Danielle.

'Hi, Danielle – I'm ringing to ask a favour,' I said.

'Oh yes? What kind of favour? Is this still about Neeta?'

'Yes – I wondered if you could ask around at the Uni, see if anyone remembers Neeta mentioning a Rick, Craig or Dan.'

'You've got some suspects then?' said Danielle, laughing.

She clearly wasn't taking me at all seriously.

'Yes,' I said, 'possible suspects, anyway.'

She agreed to ask around but I wasn't totally convinced that she would.

It was only when I went to put the cordless phone back on the base, that I noticed there were three messages on the answer phone. I played them.

'*Message one: Wednesday four fourteen pm*: Michael? Are you there? It's Mum. Where are you? Michael? Pick up the phone.' There was a sighing sound. 'Michael – give me a call on my mobile when you get this message.'

'*Message two: Wednesday four thirty-eight pm*: Michael? Are you still not back? You promised to tell me if you were going anywhere after school. Call me.'

'*Message three: Wednesday five seventeen pm*: Michael – I'm getting worried now. Please phone me.'

I pressed the delete button angrily. Why did she have to track my every move? If she had her way I'd be wearing one of those electronic tags.

'*All messages deleted*,' said the machine.

I was about to ring Mum's mobile when I heard the key in the door.

Mum came in with some bags of shopping and Jamie followed, carrying more shopping.

Mum glared at me. I turned to go upstairs.

'Michael – come back here this minute,' she called. 'I want a word.'

'Okay if I go and do my homework?' said Jamie, dumping his bags on the kitchen table.

'Yes, love – Michael can help me put this lot away.'

'I've got homework too,' I protested as Jamie pushed past me.

'And you'd be well on the way to finishing it by now if you'd come straight home and got started,' said Mum.

Reluctantly, I opened a bag of shopping and began putting the milk and yoghurts in the fridge.

'Where have you been?' asked Mum.

'It . . . it was another after school maths class. Sorry I forgot to tell you.'

'Don't lie to me!'

'I'm not!'

'I *know*, Michael. When I couldn't get hold of you I tried phoning Liam to see if you were with him. I asked about after school maths classes and he said there weren't any – hadn't been any all term.'

This threw me. 'What does Liam know?' I tried. 'He's not even in my maths class.'

Mum raised her eyebrows like she didn't believe a word I was saying. I decided it was safer to try to change the subject.

'Why did you want to get hold of me anyway?' I asked. 'What was so important?' I threw some potatoes and carrots into the vegetable trays and turned to face her.

'Go easy with those,' she warned, 'I don't want them all bruised and battered.'

'So?' I said.

She turned away from me, putting the dishwasher stuff in the cupboard under the sink. 'I went to the bank on the way home yesterday,' she said, still not looking at me, 'and took out thirty pounds in cash. This morning there was only ten left in my purse. Do you have anything to say about that?'

This was too much. My voice got higher as I spoke. *'What are you saying now? That I stole money from your purse?'*

'It was there and now it's not,' said Mum. She turned to face me, folding her arms.

'Maybe Dad took it – or someone stole it from your purse while you were out,' I suggested.

'It was gone this morning before I left the house. And I've asked your dad – he knows nothing about it.'

'Maybe it was Jamie,' I said.

'Jamie says he knows nothing about it either. He reminded me how upset you were that we gave him extra pocket money this week. I wondered if you felt we "owed" you extra too.'

'I can't believe you think I'd do that,' I said. 'I didn't take it.'

'And I'm supposed to believe you,' said Mum, 'when you were clearly lying to me about where you've been?'

'Believe what you like,' I said furiously. I moved towards the stairs. Mum grabbed my arm. 'Wait, Michael. I haven't finished with you yet.'

'Well I've finished with you,' I yelled. I pulled my arm roughly away and stormed up the stairs.

Chapter 21

When Dad got home I was in more trouble. He had a right go at me and made me apologise to Mum. Of course, I still refused to say I'd taken the money, though I don't think either of them believed me. I spent most of the evening sulking in my room.

The next day at school the trouble continued. Miss Fowler had expected me to finish the maths last night and hand it in. I hadn't done it – I couldn't – not after what I'd been through. She said I'd have to have a double lot of extra homework for the weekend – and, would you believe it – I was to write her a letter of apology too!

At break I was walking towards the loos when I sensed someone watching me. I turned to see Sean Finch standing leaning against the wall. He was staring straight at me, smirking. Normally I'd have turned away and kept walking but today I was in a bad mood.

I walked back towards him, trying to keep my eyes on his.

'What are you staring at?' I demanded.

I soon realised this was not the best thing to have said.

'Not sure...' he said. He looked me up and down thoughtfully, screwing up his nose as if in disgust. 'I think it could be rodent but then again maybe it's an alien species. It's too stupid and clumsy to be a mouse – even a Mickey Mouse – I think.'

'Haven't you got something better to do with your

time than staring at me?' I asked.

'It's a free country, isn't it? I can look at what I like, can't I?'

He pressed his face right up against mine so close I could taste his foul breath.

I moved back, shaking my head. 'You're weird, Sean.'

He laughed. 'You should watch what you say, Mickey. Or you might find yourself in a mousetrap one of these days.' He clapped his hands together loudly.

I left him, still standing staring at me, and headed for the loos.

My mood didn't improve when I got to history. It turned out I'd written down the wrong page of the book in my homework diary and I'd slogged my guts out on the wrong work altogether. Mr Marshall is usually cool but he was not at all cool about this. He said I had to do the right work as well as this week's homework and hand it all in on Monday.

I managed to grab a moment with Shamila at lunchtime but that didn't go too well either.

'I went back to the playground yesterday,' I told her. 'I talked to Amy – and her sister.'

'Leave it, Michael, there's no point,' Shamila said sharply.

'Don't you want to hear what they said?'

'No – not unless they told you who killed Neeta. They didn't tell you that, did they?'

'Not exactly – but I know that photo was stuck on their fridge with a magnet and then it disappeared. And I've got some names of people who could've taken it . . .'

Shamila shook her head, holding out her hands to stop

me. 'I don't want to know, Michael. The photo probably had nothing to do with it anyway. I want you to stop trying to play detective. It's a waste of time.'

She must've seen my disappointment because her voice softened.

'Look, it's nice of you to try to help but I want you to stop now – okay?'

'But... but...'

She turned and walked away.

I couldn't believe she wasn't even grateful that I'd gone back there. It seemed like she'd given up hope. I'd have to show her, prove to her that I wasn't messing about.

The next day was Friday and Mrs Deakin called me over in registration. 'Can you come and see me at break?' she asked.

I looked at her suspiciously. 'Why, Miss?'

She smiled. 'It's nothing to worry about, Michael. I want a chat with you that's all.'

What was *that* all about? At break, I found Mrs Deakin looking flustered outside the staffroom.

'Yes, Michael? What is it?' she said.

'You asked me to come and see you,' I reminded her.

'Oh yes,' she said, tapping her head. 'Silly me – I forgot. Too many things on my mind at once. Come on then.'

I followed her into an empty classroom.

'Sit down then, this won't take long.'

I sat nervously on the edge of a chair and she perched on the table.

'Michael,' she said, sighing, 'I'm not going to beat about the bush. Your work and behaviour have deteriorated recently. Several of your teachers have mentioned it to me.

I want to know – is there something troubling you?'

I squirmed in the chair. Something troubling me – too right, there was – but I couldn't tell her. No way.

'If there is,' she continued, 'I do wish you'd tell me. This isn't like you. I've always been so impressed with the effort you've put in. I know your dyspraxia means you have to work harder than a lot of others but you are an intelligent boy...'

She paused. I looked at the floor, twiddled my thumbs and said nothing. She was so kind, her voice so gentle, that for a moment I wished I could tell her everything. But it wasn't as if she could do anything, change anything that had happened. It was my problem to sort out.

'Let me ask you straight out, Michael,' she said, leaning forward. 'Are you being bullied? It's nothing to be ashamed of if you are. But unless you tell me, I can't do anything to help.'

She paused again. I glanced up to catch her concerned frown.

'It's all right, Miss. I'm not being bullied.' I wasn't – not unless you counted being stared at by Sean Finch.

There was a long pause. I reckoned she didn't believe me. It's not like I haven't been bullied before – in Year Seven it was really bad.

'Is it...something to do with your brother starting here?' she asked.

'How do you mean?' I asked, puzzled.

'I know he's very talented musically and I imagine he finds his schoolwork easier than you as well. I only ask because I know how competitive things can get between siblings.'

'It's not that, Miss,' I said, shaking my head. 'I know I can't compete with Jamie. There's no point even trying to do that.'

Mrs Deakin sighed again. 'I've seen it happen. I knew a girl who could run off an A grade essay in half an hour while her older brother took two hours and only got a D. Resentment built up in him – it was bound to.'

'So what happened?' I asked, curious.

'Despite all the encouragement we gave him, the boy stopped trying. He was bright enough and could have done well but he simply gave up – and he still has a chip on his shoulder as if the world owes him something.'

Mrs Deakin had a wistful expression.

'Are they still at the school?' I asked.

'No, Michael – the ones I'm talking about left school a long time ago. But I'm sure there are plenty of others in a similar position now. I wouldn't want you deciding you "couldn't be bothered to work" just because you feel you can't compete with Jamie. You're very bright. Please don't let it go to waste.'

I felt my face reddening.

'Michael?' Mrs Deakin was waiting for a response. I had to say something.

'Sorry, Miss. I'll try harder from now on.'

'I'm pleased to hear it,' she said, touching my shoulder gently. 'And if you do ever want to talk about anything – you know where I am.'

'Thanks, Miss.'

Mrs Deakin stood up and smoothed her skirt. 'All right – off you go now.'

*

130

At lunchtime I had the exercise class. I thought I was feeling okay but as I started throwing a ball at the skittles my aim was all over the place.

'Come on, Michael, your scores were better last week,' said Shamila. 'Every week until now you've improved but this week's scores are going down. What's wrong?'

'I don't know. Maybe I should leave it for today. I'm not in the mood.'

'I'm not having you giving up,' said Shamila.

I looked at her in surprise.

'Why shouldn't I give up?' I argued. 'I mean, you've given up, haven't you? Given up trying to find out about Neeta.'

Her face fell. 'That's different. There's nothing I can do about that – whereas there's plenty you can do about this. You need to try harder, that's all.'

'We could try harder – together – to find out about Neeta.'

I saw her shoulders tense. 'No, Michael. It's kind of you to want to help but there's no point, is there? I want to do things to take my mind off it. My aunt and uncle have gone back home now – that's something. It's too painful to think about all the time – you see that, don't you? Start dribbling that ball. Mr Bates is watching us.'

'But ... maybe if you knew – who did it, and why,' I argued, 'you'd be able to think about it less – and concentrate more on your work and that.'

Shamila stood up and kicked the ball towards me. It went flying past.

I hurried to catch it up and dribbled it back towards her.

'Shamila, I'm sorry. I shouldn't have brought it up.'

I continued with the exercises in silence while she counted and wrote down my scores.

'That's a bit better,' she said, finally, 'but still not as good as last week.'

'Listen,' I said, 'I wondered...it's my birthday this Sunday.'

'Is it?' she said, without looking up.

'Me and a few mates, we're going to the cinema, to see that new action film. It's meant to be good. You know...you said you want to take your mind off things – well, I wondered if, maybe...you might like to come. What do you think?'

I held my breath. I hadn't thought I'd have the guts to ask her. I loved the idea of her being there – Shamila by my side, watching the film. But I wasn't sure how it'd be with all my mates there as well. Liam had been making a big enough thing about me and Shamila as it was.

To be honest, I knew I'd rather go just with Shamila, but that wouldn't be fair on my mates – I couldn't leave them out on my birthday. I didn't think Shamila would say yes anyway, but I'd dreamt of asking her – and now I had. My heart was beating fast. I wished I hadn't said anything about Neeta. I'd put her in a bad mood. Maybe because of that, she'd say no.

'You could bring Kelly – or Leanne if you want,' I added, 'so it's not just you and a bunch of boys.'

'Thanks for asking,' Shamila said, 'but it's not my kind of film.'

'No worries,' I said, partly disappointed and partly relieved. It was only later I thought, why hadn't I said,

'Maybe we could see a different film another night?' Would she have said yes to that?

I felt like I had to prove myself first and the only way I could do that was by finding out who murdered Neeta. Then she'd take me seriously – want to be with me – wouldn't she?

Chapter 22

On Saturday morning I arrived early at the swimming pool and waited outside for Danielle. She came hurrying anxiously along the pavement, a few minutes late.

'Don't worry,' I said, 'I haven't been waiting long.'

She looked back along the road, distractedly.

'What's the matter?' I asked.

'I don't know. It's probably nothing – but I felt like someone was following me just now.'

'Following you?' I repeated.

'Yes. Before I turned the corner I heard footsteps behind me but when I looked back there was no one there. The weird thing is – this isn't the first time. Yesterday I thought someone was following me too, when I got off the bus at Uni. I caught a glimpse of someone, then he shot off down a side turning.'

'Do you want me to go and look?' I said. 'See if he's still hanging about?'

'No, it's probably nothing,' she said. She made a feeble attempt at a brave smile but it didn't conceal her anxiety one bit. 'I expect I was imagining it – but I'm telling you, Michael, it's given me the creeps – especially after what happened to Neeta. I can't say anything to Mum and Dad or they'd freak out – and not let me go anywhere on my own at all. That'd be a nightmare – and it's probably nothing, as I said.'

We walked inside.

'Have you managed to ask around,' I asked, 'about Rick, Dan or Craig?'

'Yes – I did. But no luck, I'm afraid. Only one girl remembers seeing Neeta with a man but she doesn't know his name. She can't even remember what he looked like. See you in a minute.'

She disappeared into the ladies' changing room. I made my way to the men's. As I got changed, I had a scary thought. Could there be a connection between Danielle asking around about Rick, Craig or Dan, and her thinking she was being followed today? What if someone who knew something had overheard and thought Danielle was getting too close to the truth? I didn't want to even consider this as a possibility.

When we were changed and in the water, I was eager to practise swimming but Danielle wanted to teach me to tread water.

'Once you can tread water, you'll be able to relax more when you're swimming. Come on – it'll be easier if you go out of your depth – then you won't have the temptation to put your feet down.'

I wasn't sure about this.

'Don't worry – I'll stay close enough to help out if need be.'

I moved along the bar about halfway up the length of the pool. Danielle followed.

'How deep is it here?' I asked, nervously.

'Deep enough. Don't worry – you'll be fine.'

She demonstrated and then encouraged me to push away from the side and have a go. I was doing well – but when I looked round I realised I was now much further from the side of the pool than I thought. And I couldn't see Danielle. I suddenly panicked and my arms began thrashing wildly, in an effort to stay up. I tried to call out but my mouth filled with water. I could feel myself going under. I twisted and rolled, feeling completely disoriented. Where was Danielle?

It was then that I felt hands grabbing me – but my relief turned to further panic when I realised the hands were pushing me down – not pulling me up. It was my nightmare – my nightmare come real. I struggled frantically, trying to pull myself away but the hands held on tight, refused to budge. This was it, I thought. I was going to die.

I felt a lurch as I was pulled backwards, down further so I thought any moment I must hit the bottom of the pool. Instead, with a shock, I found my head breaking the surface. Air – at last – I gasped for breath, spluttering, my body shaking uncontrollably.

The blurred shape of Danielle was in front of me. She guided me towards the bar at the edge of the pool, and I edged slowly along until my feet could touch the bottom securely.

'Thanks,' I puffed, when I had enough breath. Then with panic I swung round, terrified – remembering my attacker. 'Where is he? Is he still here?' I gasped.

'Is who still here? What happened, Michael? Were you deliberately trying to drown yourself, and me too?'

'Of course not – but someone was pushing me under – you must've seen.'

'Pushing you under?' said Danielle. 'I was trying to pull you up. It was me, Michael – no one else – but you were struggling so much you made it very difficult.'

136

She rubbed her arm which was clearly red from where I'd tried to pull away.

'I'm getting out,' I said, wading towards the steps.

'It's all right, Michael – you were doing well. You can stay in the shallow end if you like. What's the matter?'

'I can't do it,' I said. 'I'm going to get changed.'

'Michael, wait.'

I ignored her, shivering as I stumbled along the slippery poolside, nearly losing my footing. But I made it to the men's changing room. I was still shaking so much it took me ages to get dry and dressed. Danielle even sent a steward in to check I was okay.

When I finally came out, she was sitting at a table in the foyer, sipping a coffee. I felt so embarrassed and confused about what had happened, I couldn't face the idea of talking about it with her.

'I'm going home,' I said, hurrying past, towards the door.

'Michael, wait,' she said, standing up, 'please.'

I hesitated.

'Come and sit down for a minute. You look all shaky. And you'd better do up your flies before you go anywhere.'

I did my flies hastily and sat down. She was right, I was still shaking.

'I think you must have had some kind of panic attack in the pool,' said Danielle. 'You scared me, Michael. What was going on in your head?'

'I ... I've been having nightmares,' I said quietly, ' – about drowning, someone pushing me under. In the pool ... I felt like it was really happening.'

Danielle frowned. 'I wish you'd told me about the nightmares before,' she said. 'When did they start?'

I shrugged. 'A while ago. Before I started lessons with you.'

'It was brave of you to ask for swimming lessons, then,' she said. 'I wonder what the dreams meant. Have you any idea?'

'You're not gonna start psychoanalysing me?' I said, half jokey, half fearful.

'Of course not,' she said. 'I hope I didn't make things worse, talking about my phantom stalker.'

'No – it was nothing to do with that. I thought if I learnt to swim, maybe the nightmares would stop, that's all. But they haven't – I was wrong. I can't do it. Nothing in the world is going to get me in a swimming pool again.'

Danielle shook her head. 'If you give up now, then you're giving in to the nightmares – aren't you? They're bound to carry on.'

'At least I wake up from them and I'm safe in bed – I'm not going to drown, like I nearly did just now. Anyway, I don't want to talk about it anymore. I'm going home.'

I stood up and walked towards the door.

'Michael – don't go,' she called after me, but this time I kept walking.

Chapter 23

Back at home, I slogged away at my homework all afternoon. My writing in my maths book was messier than ever and even my essay on 'The Slave Trade' for history was full of mistakes. I wasn't sure why I was even bothering.

Sunday was my birthday. Why are birthdays always crap? I guess it's because you think it's going to be extra-special and it never works out like that – not for me, anyway.

It started with a phone call. Mum yelled at me to answer it. She said it was probably Gran or Grandad phoning to wish me happy birthday. But it wasn't. It was someone breathing, heavily, like before. No one spoke. Could it be Liam or someone trying to wind me up? Surely not – not on my birthday. But who was it?

The phone clicked. I did 1471. The caller had withheld their number. Could it have been Tanya – or could she have known more than she'd said – and passed my phone number on to someone else? At the back of my mind was the thought that someone knew what I'd seen by the canal. Someone knew and they were trying to intimidate me – warn me off – and maybe Danielle too.

At breakfast, I tried to forget about it and focus on my presents. I got a new mobile phone from Mum and Dad.

Mum had chosen the one with the biggest buttons so it'd be easier for me but it made it a lot less cool-looking. At least no one would want to steal it.

Jamie gave me a book which I'm sure I recognised as one someone had given him for his last birthday. I was disappointed but I tried to sound pleased.

I ended up doing some more homework in the morning, even though I'd been determined not to. I was nowhere near finished – and was still nowhere near finished by lunchtime. I was beginning to feel depressed.

Over lunch, Mum asked me what was wrong.

'Nothing,' I said.

'It's your birthday – you should be happy,' she said.

Maybe that's the trouble with birthdays – everyone, including yourself, thinking you should be happy, so you feel bad if you're not.

I tried to cheer myself up when the others came over later. We went for pizza and to the cinema. The film was excellent. I knew I was going to like it from the moment it started. The special effects were amazing and there were some mega-scary parts. It was more of a thriller than a straight action film.

Then, that night I had the swimming nightmare again – only it was all mixed up with the characters in the film. I woke up covered in sweat but at least I hadn't woken Mum this time.

On Monday morning Shamila came up to me in the playground and pushed an envelope into my hand. For a moment I thought it was something to do with Neeta but as I opened it I realised it was a birthday card. Shamila

140

had actually cared enough to get me a birthday card! She must like me a bit, then – surely? She'd even written, '*with love, Shamila*'. Love!

'Sorry it's a day late,' she said. 'I'd have posted it but I don't know your address. Did you have a nice birthday?'

'It was okay, I suppose. It would've been better if you'd been there.'

She smiled.

'Look,' I said, 'I got a new mobile. I'll give you the number if you like.'

She nodded, took out her phone and we keyed in each other's numbers. It felt cool, having Shamila's number in my phone. Her mobile was half the size of mine but she didn't laugh or anything.

I also felt even more determined to solve Neeta's murder. I owed it to Shamila. But what could I do? I still had no idea if the photo was even important but I didn't have much in the way of other clues.

In the end, I decided I'd drop in on Elsie. I had told her I'd come back – and maybe I could jog her memory – and find out something else useful. I wasn't giving up, even if Shamila had. I texted Mum to say I was going to visit an old people's home after school as part of a project. Well, it was a project, wasn't it? Just not a school one.

Elsie was sitting in the same chair in the lounge. It was as if she hadn't moved since my last visit. Her face lit up when she saw me. I was pleased I'd come and felt guilty for not having been back sooner. I pulled a chair over and sat down opposite her.

'How's the detective work going?' she whispered, giving me a furtive wink.

I shrugged. 'Not that well. I keep thinking I've got a lead but where it leads is nowhere, if you see what I mean.'

'I was hoping you'd come back,' she said, leaning forward. 'I thought of something, after you'd gone – something that might be of interest, but I had no way of getting in touch with you.'

'What was it?' I asked eagerly, wishing now that I'd come back sooner.

'It was that photo you showed me made me think of it – that little girl. I know I thought I recognised that playground but I could've been wrong. Lots of playgrounds look the same, I suppose.'

'But it was the right playground,' I told her. 'I've been there twice since you suggested it and I've met the girl in the photo. Her name's Amy. It's definitely her. I don't know how Neeta ended up with her photo though. She never mentioned an "Amy" to you, did she?'

'Amy? No – I don't think so,' said Elsie. 'You've confused me now. You see, when I thought about it, I remembered something Neeta told me, and it would've made sense – her having that photo in her bag. But it can't be – not if it was that playground . . . How strange.'

'What did you remember?' I asked. 'You might as well tell me anyway.'

Elsie looked doubtful but I leaned forward encouragingly.

'Well . . . it happened last year, if I remember right, back home before she came to university. Neeta said she used to babysit for a neighbour's little girl – sweet kid, so she said – I can't remember the name – but I don't think it was Amy, no. And one day, when she was taking her to the park, the poor little mite got knocked down by a car.'

'What – were they crossing the road?' I asked.

'No, the car came right up on the pavement out of nowhere, I'm sure that's what Neeta said. Hit-and-run – the driver didn't even stop. The poor kid died before the ambulance got her to hospital.'

'That's awful.'

Elsie sighed and rubbed her eyes. She shook her head, sadly. 'Tragedy it was. Neeta was practically in tears when she told me – and it brought tears to my eyes too, like it has now, telling you. Neeta said she got ever so depressed after it happened. It's not surprising, is it?'

I shook my head. So that was why Neeta was so depressed. I wondered if Shamila knew – she'd certainly never mentioned it.

'But of course everyone's sympathy was with the family, the little girl's parents and her sister. Neeta felt that no one understood how badly it had affected her. She felt guilty too, even though the car had swerved onto the pavement – it wasn't as if she could have done anything. She felt like the family were blaming her – and who knows, maybe they were.'

'Must've been terrible for her,' I said, as Elsie paused for breath.

'Neeta sank into depression – that's what she told me – wished it was her that had been killed and not the child. She felt so bad, she thought she'd never get through her A-levels or make it to university. And she couldn't usually bear to talk about it – she said there was something special about me – that she felt she could tell me.'

'Thanks for telling me about it,' I said. 'It explains why Neeta was depressed even if it doesn't help much with solving the murder. She must have kept very quiet about it. I'm sure Shamila, Neeta's cousin, didn't know or she would have said something.'

'You see, after you were here,' said Elsie, 'I thought maybe that little girl in the photo was the one who got knocked down. But if you've met her then it couldn't have been, could it? I mean – that little girl's dead. Not much help at all, am I?' said Elsie, sighing.

'Yes – you've been great,' I told her. 'I'm sure we'd never have found Amy if it wasn't for you recognising the playground.'

We sat in slightly awkward silence for a few minutes.

'Neeta never mentioned a Rick, Dan or Craig to you, did she?' I asked.

Elsie looked thoughtful. 'Her boyfriend, do you mean?'

'I don't know – why? I didn't think she had one.'

'I think she might have done,' said Elsie. 'I'm not sure, to be honest. She certainly went off from here to meet someone once or twice. I think it was a boy because she used to go to the bathroom and do up her face and put a bit of perfume on before she left. She never said anything, mind. I don't recognise any of those names.'

'No worries,' I said. 'But – in case you do think of anything, can I give you my mobile phone number?'

'If you like, dear.'

Once I'd given her the number we both went quiet again. It seemed rude to go so soon but I wasn't sure what else to say. Then I spotted a game of dominoes on the shelf. I picked it up. 'Would you like a game?' I asked her.

It was on my way home, churning things over in my mind, that I had a completely new idea for the murder motive. What if Neeta had seen or knew the man who'd knocked the girl down in the car? What if she was too scared to say? What if the man had tracked Neeta down and killed her to make sure she didn't say anything? The more I thought about it, the more convinced I was that this was a possibility.

At least I'd left Elsie my mobile number now, so if she thought of anything else she could tell me straight away.

Chapter 24

The next day in the corridor at school I grabbed a moment with Shamila.

'I went to see Elsie yesterday,' I told her.

Shamila looked both annoyed and puzzled. 'Michael, I told you to stop playing detective. This isn't a game. Anyway, you already talked to her so why go there again?'

'She doesn't get many visitors,' I said. 'I'd told her I'd come back, so I went, okay?'

'Sorry,' she said. 'As long as you weren't there to question her more.'

'Do you know why Neeta was so depressed?' I asked.

Shamila shrugged. 'I don't know for sure but I still reckon she thought she had cancer. Even if she hadn't told her doctor, I think that must have been on her mind. It's the only explanation for her having that cancer research centre phone number.'

'So your family haven't told you the real reason?' I said.

'What are you on about, Michael? Spit it out, will you? Break'll be over and I want to go to the loo before maths.'

'Elsie told me something yesterday – something that Neeta told her.'

'What?'

I explained about the hit-and-run accident and the little girl who'd been killed.

Shamila looked shocked and hurt. 'If that's true, then why didn't anyone tell me about it?'

'Maybe Neeta asked her parents not to say anything to yours. Elsie said she didn't generally like to talk about it.'

Shamila bit her fingernails. 'It doesn't make any difference though, does it?' she said, her voice flatter. 'It can't have anything to do with the murder.'

'That's where you're wrong,' I said smugly.

'What do you mean?'

'It was a hit-and-run, right? What if Neeta either saw or knew who did it? Maybe the person wanted to kill her to make sure she kept quiet.'

Shamila looked thoughtful.

'Well?' I said.

'It can't have been that,' said Shamila.

I looked at her in surprise. 'How do you know it can't?'

Shamila hesitated. 'There was money missing from Neeta's bank account – all her student loan money and some of her savings too. That doesn't fit in with your theory, does it?'

'Money missing?' I repeated. I was angry now. 'Why didn't you tell me this before?'

'I didn't tell you because I didn't want you to start coming up with new theories and investigating them. And I only found out yesterday, as it happens. I overheard Mum and Dad talking about it. I didn't catch all of it – but the police found out Dad has extra money in his account that he couldn't explain. They think there's some connection.'

'And is there?' I asked. 'What did your dad say?'

'He told Mum the money came from clients he was doing extra work for on the side. He was working on his own as well as for the company – which isn't allowed. But he was still making more for the company than most of the other staff. He didn't want to get the clients into trouble so he didn't tell the police. Mum said he should tell them but Dad was angry – he said, why should the police think Neeta had been giving him money?'

'What's your theory, then – about the missing money?'

'I don't have a theory, Michael,' Shamila snapped.

At that moment, Sean Finch appeared, sauntering along the corridor like he owned the place.

'Mickey, what you doing hanging round with that dirty Paki girl?' he said.

I was shocked. I felt Shamila bristling next to me. I couldn't believe he'd said that – especially when he knew what had happened to Shamila's cousin. Sean stood still, his eyes challenging me to respond.

I guess all the tension of the weeks since that moment by the canal – and all my feelings for Shamila – just took over at that moment. I didn't think. I swung my right fist at him. He dodged, surprised. I swung again, before he had time to react. My aim wasn't good. It was hard enough for me to know where my fist would end up, let alone him. He guessed wrong. I caught him, right in the face, much harder than I had expected. He reeled back, stunned, his hand over his left eye. I reeled back too, my hand hurting from the impact. I was almost as stunned as he was. I'm not one to start a fight – not me – especially not with Sean Finch.

'Michael!' Shamila squeaked, pulling at my arm.

I looked up. Sean was flying at me in a rage. I knew I was in for it. I closed my eyes, shielding my face with my hands. The blow came fast and hard, and I couldn't stop myself falling. I tried to sit up but he was on top of me, still thumping me, my chest, head, everywhere.

Then a loud woman's voice yelled, 'Sean Finch! Stop that this instant!'

It was Mrs Deakin.

I opened my eyes. She had grabbed Sean by the back of his jumper and pulled him up.

'Weren't me,' Sean complained. 'He started it.'

'Save it for the Head,' said Mrs Deakin. 'Are you all right, Michael? Can you stand up?'

Mrs Deakin took my arm and helped me to my feet.

'I'm fine,' I told her, though I felt bruised and battered.

'Both of you – outside Mr Mortimer's office now. We'll see what he has to say about this.'

Sean and I stood in the Head's office with heads bowed, while he demanded an explanation. I expected Sean to repeat his accusation that I'd started it but he was silent, so I kept quiet too. Maybe he realised Mr Mortimer would never believe him. Maybe he thought he'd lose street cred if it got out that I'd started a fight with him.

After a while, the Head told Sean to go to Miss Wood to have his eye seen to. After Sean had left the room, he beckoned me to sit down.

'If you're having trouble with Sean, you must tell us so that we can deal with it properly. Violence is not the answer.'

'It was a one-off, Sir. It won't happen again,' I said.

'I certainly hope not,' said the Head. 'But I'm afraid I will have to inform your parents.

'Do you have to?' I asked, in horror.

'Yes, Michael – I do.'

After school I went home to face the music. That's a good joke, isn't it! My house full of musicians! There was no joking at home.

'Look at the state of you!' Mum exclaimed. 'Fighting! I told Mr Mortimer that he must be mistaken. Perhaps it was another boy called Michael, I told him. My Michael doesn't behave like that. But he says it was definitely you. He thought Sean might be bullying you. Is he? What's got into you, Michael? What's going on?'

I shrugged, which made Mum even angrier.

'That's not good enough. I want an explanation,' said Mum.

'I was walking along the corridor with this girl,' I said. 'Her name's Shamila and she's Asian, right? Then Sean Finch came along and called her a "dirty Paki". She was really upset, I could tell. So I hit him.'

'Very gallant, I'm sure,' said Mum. 'But there's no excuse for violence.'

'That's what Mr Mortimer said, but what was I supposed to do?'

'You could have told Sean that wasn't a nice thing to say and suggest that he apologise to the girl.'

'He'd have hit me for sure if I'd said that!' I told her.

'Looks to me like he did a good job of hitting you anyway,' she said. 'You should have told a teacher and let them deal with him.'

150

I sighed. She didn't have a clue.

'I feel so ashamed, Michael,' Mum continued. 'And Mr Mortimer says your school work has gone downhill and you've been forgetting homework. We're going to have to go back to what we did when you were in Year Seven. We'll sit down after school, your dad or I, and we'll go through your homework diary with you and help you to organise your time.'

'Oh Mum, I don't need you to do that.'

'From what Mr Mortimer says, it sounds like you do.'

Later that evening, after Mum had checked my homework diary and gone through my homework to make sure I'd done it properly, I was feeling totally fed up. Then the phone rang.

'It's for you, Michael!' Mum called.

I picked up the phone. 'Hello?'

It was a girl's voice. 'Is that Michael?' she said.

'Yes, who is it?' I asked.

'It's Tanya.'

'Oh – hi,' I said in surprise. 'You haven't tried to ring before, have you?'

'No.'

'Or given my number to anyone else?' I added.

'No, of course not. D'you wanna hear what I gotta say or what?'

'Sorry – go on then.'

'I rang you 'cos I thought you might wanna know.' She paused.

'Know what?' I demanded.

'About Craig. He was 'ere the other day. He was a

right mess. Looked like someone had done him in. He was trying to get money off me mum.'

My mind whirled. Money – the missing money. What if Neeta was secretly going out with this Craig – and he'd convinced her to give him money – or lend it, maybe? She could've refused to give him anymore and that's why he killed her. But would you kill someone over something like that?

'Where does this Craig live?' I asked Tanya.

'I dunno,' she said. 'He lived 'ere for a bit but I dunno where he lives now.'

My heart sank. What use was that?

'You still there?' she asked.

'Yeah.'

'I know where he hangs out,' said Tanya, 'or where he used to, anyway. The King's Head pub – on North Street. D'you know it?'

'Yes – I think so.'

'Mum used to meet him there sometimes when they was going out. He's got a temper though – so you better watch it. That's why Mum dumped him – that and the money.'

'Thanks,' I said.

'It's no bother,' said Tanya, 'but Craig weren't never interested in me or Amy so I don't think he'd want her photo, would he?'

'Thanks anyway,' I said, 'it was good of you to bother to ring.'

'S'all right,' she said. 'When do I get the reward?'

Chapter 25

My heart was pounding when I came off the phone. The man *was* Craig. Craig was the man. It was definite. I was sure he was the one who'd taken the photo and I knew he was the one who'd killed Neeta. All I wanted was to get enough evidence to go to the police without having to admit that I'd seen the fight. I needed to know how he knew Neeta – and why he'd killed her. How had a sensible girl like Neeta got involved with a nasty piece of work like Craig? And why would she have agreed to give him money?

First things first – I had to go to the King's Head and hover about in the hope that he'd turn up there.

'I'm going to Liam's,' I told Dad. He'd only just come in so I was hoping he hadn't had a chance to talk to Mum. I was wrong.

'No, Michael, you're not going anywhere – not after fighting at school and forgetting to do your homework, not to mention lying about the money and where you were the other day. You're grounded for the rest of the week.'

'But, Dad – I've finished my homework tonight. Mum's checked it and everything. She never said I was grounded. I didn't take Mum's money – and the fight wasn't all my fault. I've got a right to a life, haven't I?'

'No,' said Dad. 'And that's final.'

'But, Dad – you're treating me like a little kid – I'm fourteen.'

153

'Then start acting in a more adult way.'

I gave in. Then, to make matters worse, I had to put up with Mum pestering me about the girl on the phone.

'Is she your girlfriend?' Mum asked. 'Is that who you've been spending time with – why you're being so secretive? Is she from school? She sounded a bit... a bit coarse – the way she spoke...'

'Mum! You're a snob, you are. Why are you judging someone by the way they speak? And she's not my girlfriend anyway. Leave me alone.'

I spent the evening and the following evenings acting as moody and sulky as possible. I was hoping that they'd tell me to go out just to get rid of me. It didn't work.

The next day at school I was scared that Sean would be after me to get his own back but to my relief I discovered he'd been excluded for a week. Apparently he'd been on a final warning for fighting. I had a minuscule moment of guilt – after all, I had started the fight even if he had provoked me. I'd got off lightly compared to him – but then I'd never been caught fighting before. Anyway, I wasn't about to feel guilty for long. Enough people had suffered at his hands. He deserved it, especially after what he'd called Shamila.

'Is it true? Did you hit Sean Finch?' Nick asked me in the corridor.

I nodded. 'Yeah.'

'Wow! I didn't think you had the guts for that. I mean – *Sean Finch!* Nobody messes with him.'

I felt a moment of pride. 'I can hardly believe I did it,' I admitted to Nick.

154

'You're gonna have to watch your back now,' warned Nick, shuddering.

'But Sean's been excluded – haven't you heard?'

'Yes – and I bet he's none too pleased.'

As we entered our form room I looked over towards Shamila. She glanced up but didn't meet my eyes. Surely she was grateful? She must've seen I had guts to do what I did – and I did it for her, after all. I tried to talk to her on the way to first lesson – but she was clearly avoiding me.

I was grounded until Saturday. I tried to persuade Mum and Dad to let me off but they wouldn't budge. It wasn't fair. I had more important things to do than sit around at home. I thought I'd be okay on Thursday because Mum and Dad would both be at rehearsals. But they took it in turns to keep phoning me to make sure I was in. The only good thing about being grounded was that I couldn't accidentally bump into Sean Finch when I was wandering the streets.

On Friday Shamila didn't have lunch with me but she did come to the exercise class. She marked my scores but not with her usual enthusiasm. I tried to talk to her about Sean. She said she'd liked me because she thought I was kind and gentle and not the sort to get violent. I said I never had before and that I'd done it for her. She said, 'Next time don't bother.'

That night Danielle rang me to see if I was coming swimming. I refused point blank.

'No way,' I told her and she didn't try to persuade me. I was surprised but then she said,

'I don't mind tomorrow. As it happens a gorgeous guy

has invited me to go out with him for the day. I told him I wouldn't be free until lunchtime but now we can head off earlier.'

'Oh yeah?' I teased.

'But I think we should meet for a swimming lesson next weekend, otherwise the longer you leave it the harder it will get.'

'I'll think about it,' I told her.

Instead, on Saturday I had a lie-in and then, finally allowed out of the house, I headed off to the King's Head pub around lunchtime. At least it was easy to find. And there was a café across the road where I could sit unnoticed and watch. Not many people were going in or out of the pub. Maybe it wasn't a good time. Sunday might be better.

I made my mug of hot chocolate last for as long as I could. But after a while it was empty and I was bored. I left the café and walked up and down the road. This was a waste of time. I might have to come back tomorrow or one evening after school. It might even take days of waiting around here before I'd catch up with him. And Tanya might be wrong – he might not even drink at that pub anymore.

As I went past the Bookies for the second time, two men came out, one of them talking loudly to the other. I froze. He wasn't limping anymore but I recognised his jacket and his voice. It was Craig.

I slipped back into a shop doorway so he wouldn't see me. The other man went into the King's Head but Craig was heading for the bus stop. A bus was pulling up.

Without hesitating I ran and followed him onto it. I sat down, breathless, a few seats behind him. I knew I had to do a better job of following him than I had with that man near the swimming pool. I also didn't want him recognising me from the alley. This man was dangerous. This man had killed.

The people sitting in front of me got off at the next stop. Now, if Craig turned round he could easily see me. I began to panic. I tried telling myself that even if he did see me and recognise me there was no reason why he'd think it wasn't coincidence. I happened to be on the same bus as him, that's all. But the panicky feeling wouldn't go. I kept my head down, half hiding my face with my hand, but glancing up every few seconds to check he was still there.

He went five stops, then got off. Two people across the aisle stood up to get off as well so I didn't look too conspicuous as I followed. Craig walked slowly up the main road and turned down a side turning. I followed at a distance and then hurried to reach the side turning in case he turned again but he was still there. He went up the driveway of the fourth house along, pulled a key from his pocket and went in. I continued past, making a mental note of the house number – seven.

It was easier than I could possibly have hoped.

I heard the door shut and after a few seconds' wait, I turned back, and walked to the junction, where I noted the street name, Chestnut Close. I took a deep breath as I crossed the main road and walked to the bus stop. I had found the murderer! I knew his name, I knew he'd been short of money and I knew where he lived. Now all I needed to know was why he'd killed Neeta.

Chapter 26

On Sunday afternoon I had a major row with Mum. She was checking over my English homework and she said I ought to completely redo it.

'No way,' I told her. I'd spent ages on it. I knew it wasn't brilliant but it was okay. No way was I starting again. I ended up swearing at Mum and she flew off the handle at me, ranting and raging and saying I had no respect and she didn't know what had got into me.

I stormed out of the house before she could ground me again. I went round to Liam's but his mum said he was at his dad's. I tried phoning Nick and Darren but they were busy too. No one seemed to have any time for me. In the end, I went to see Elsie. I didn't know what else to do. Weirdly, she was the one person I knew would be pleased to see me.

Everyone in the lounge at Springview was still sitting in the same seats as my earlier two visits. Elsie looked different though – her hair was tightly curled.

'You've had your hair done,' I commented.

Elsie smiled, touching her hair. 'Yes – do you like it?'

'It's lovely.'

'I had a wonderful hairdresser where I used to live,' Elsie continued, 'a real diamond, she was. But you don't get any choice here – just Maggie, and she's not the best. It's better than nothing, I suppose.'

Elsie sighed. I pulled over a stool and sat down.

'I hope you don't feel like you have to keep coming here,' she said, frowning. 'You're under no obligation, you know.'

'No – it's okay. I like coming.'

Elsie smiled again. 'So what's it to be – dominoes or draughts?'

There was something safe about playing dominoes with Elsie. I brought the box over, beginning to relax. We played one game and were turning the dominoes over for another, when Elsie began to cough.

'Are you okay?' I asked anxiously. Her cough was hoarse and rasping. She didn't stop. I looked round for a member of staff but couldn't see anyone.

'Be a pet,' said Elsie, between coughs, 'and fetch me ... fetch me a glass of water from ... from the kitchen.' She was still coughing as I dashed along the corridor.

I hoped to find a staff member in the kitchen but it was empty. Hadn't anyone heard the coughing? I opened cupboards frantically, searching for a glass. Finding one, I hurried to the sink and filled it (not too full) from the tap.

I turned quickly back towards the door.

'All right there?' came a woman's voice.

She startled me. I hadn't heard her come in. I must have been edgy because I lurched. The glass slid from my hands, water flew everywhere and the glass smashed into pieces on the floor.

'I'm so sorry,' I said, looking up to see the woman who'd showed me in the first day. 'I was fetching Elsie a glass of water – she's coughing badly.' I pointed towards the lounge.

'Don't worry – I'll see to her,' said the woman. 'She gets these coughing fits sometimes.'

She stepped carefully over the broken glass and took another from the cupboard.

'I'll clear this mess,' I said, 'if you can tell me where there's a dustpan and brush.'

'Thanks – it's in there,' she said, indicating a cupboard in the hallway outside the kitchen. 'And you'll find some old newspaper there to wrap those big bits of glass. Mind your hands, won't you? I must see to Elsie.'

She filled the glass and hurried off.

I found the dustpan and brush and swept up the smaller glass fragments as carefully as I could. Then I found the bag of smelly old newspapers and pulled one out, unfolding it so I could wrap the larger pieces. A headline in the paper caught my eye.

'Locals raise money for Cancer Kid.'

There was a picture of a little boy about five years old. I skimmed through the article. It began, 'Louis Taylor's parents are grateful to our readers for their donations. They are close to reaching the sum needed for Louis to fly to the U.S. for a potentially life-saving operation. Louis has a rare form of cancer for which there is no suitable treatment in the UK.' The paper was the *Thurbridge Advertiser* and it was dated October twenty-eighth.

I re-read it, three times – gripped by it – though I wasn't sure why. There was something about it . . . I tore the article out, folded it and pushed it into my pocket, wrapping the glass fragments in the rest of the paper.

'You all right there?' said the woman, coming back

into the kitchen. 'Here – let me do that. You go back and talk to Elsie. She's fine now.'

I stood up. 'I'm really sorry about the broken glass,' I said. 'It slipped.'

'Don't worry about it,' she said.

I went back to see Elsie, who was rather red-faced but no longer coughing.

'Oh, there you are, Michael. I hope I didn't scare you,' she said.

'I was scared – a bit,' I admitted. 'What if I hadn't been here? How long does it take for one of the staff to come?'

'In a meeting, I expect,' said Elsie. 'They always seem to be in meetings. They're pleasant enough, the staff, but never around when you need them.'

'That's really bad. How did you end up here? I mean – there's no one else like you – no one you can chat to and that.'

'When I was in hospital, after my fall, they had to find somewhere quickly. I didn't have any relatives who could go round looking at places. They plonked me in the first home they found that had a space. It's comfortable enough, and as I said, the staff are pleasant. I mustn't grumble.'

'I think you should grumble,' I told her. 'Then maybe they'd find you somewhere better.'

Elsie shrugged. 'Another game?'

We played five more games of dominoes, then I thought I'd better go.

Back at home, in my room, I pulled the piece of newspaper out of my pocket and re-read the article.

Images chased each other through my mind, trying to connect. This child with cancer needing money for treatment – Neeta's picture of Amy, who didn't have cancer. Neeta having the phone number of a cancer research centre in her pocket. A man – Craig – desperate for money. A theory was growing in my mind – but could he have done something as vile as I was imagining? Was it possible? Could Craig have seen this article too?

I knew he was after money – and I knew money was missing from Neeta's account. What if this article had given Craig an idea of a way to get some money quickly? He took the photo of Amy from the fridge – and then looked around for a likely person who might be fooled. Somehow – he found Neeta.

Then he told her some sob story about this little girl in the photo – he could've made out she was his little girl – saying that she had a rare kind of cancer and needed to go to the U.S. for treatment, or she would die. It might not be that exactly – but something like that. And Neeta fell for it – and gave him the money. Would she have given money to a stranger? Maybe he'd asked her out – made her feel special – and told her about the child later.

But wait – what about the kid she used to babysit for – the one who got knocked down by a car? Neeta was full of guilt about it. Maybe she'd told Craig about it – or maybe he struck lucky. Neeta could've felt like he was giving her a chance to make amends – to save another child's life. Yes – it was possible – that might be how he got the money from her.

But why did he kill her? Especially as she had given him the money? I thought hard. Somehow she must've found out that he'd tricked her – that could be it. That might even be why she got depressed again and started feeling suicidal – because she'd been fooled. She felt too humiliated to tell anyone how she'd been tricked. Instead, she found Craig and confronted him – demanded her money back. That could've been what I'd seen them fighting about by the canal. He'd tried to warn her off – to frighten her into keeping quiet – but she wouldn't let it go. He'd got angry – gone too far – and killed her – maybe not intentionally – but she ended up dead in the canal. Could I be right? Or was my imagination going wild?

My heart was beating fast. I had to test my theory on someone – and that someone – that someone had to be Shamila.

I picked up my mobile.

'Hello?' It was wonderful to hear her voice.

'Hi, Shamila,' I said. 'I'm ringing 'cos...'

She cut me short. 'Michael – this isn't a good time.'

'That's okay – sorry, I'll ring later, shall I?'

'No...we can talk at school tomorrow, okay? I have to go.'

That was it. Before I had time to utter another word, she'd gone. I rang again but she'd switched off her phone. How could she? The disappointment hung over me like a dark cloud. Should I go to the police? It didn't feel right to go without speaking to Shamila first. She might know something that would kill my theory dead – like when she suddenly said there was money missing from Neeta's account. She might know something else she hadn't told me. But I didn't want to wait until Monday.

Chapter 27

I apologised to Mum for swearing but she was still in a mood with me. I stayed in my room most of the evening. Dad was performing and didn't get back in until late.

That night in bed, I tossed and turned, unable to sleep. My murder theory was going round and round in my head nonstop. At what must've been around midnight, I got up to go to the loo. I passed Mum and Dad's bedroom and could hear them talking. I paused to listen and heard Mum say,

'But it'd be like sending him away.'

This caught my attention – what was she on about? I stepped nearer to their door to hear better.

'He needs special teaching,' said Dad. 'You must see that – the way he is. He needs people with the best skills to get the best out of him.'

'Maybe you're right,' said Mum. 'But boarding school . . . he'll be so far away from us.'

I'd heard enough. I couldn't believe it. I was shocked. They were planning to send me away to a special school – a boarding school for kids with special needs. They hadn't even thought to ask me what I might feel about it. They were doing it without involving me at all. I felt rage welling up inside me. I wanted to burst in and yell at both of them but I daren't – I didn't want them to know I'd been eavesdropping. No way, I thought. No way are they sending me to some special needs boarding school.

I went to the loo. Tears pricked my eyes. Didn't they care? They wanted me out of the way, so they could get on with their perfect, musical lives, without me cramping their style.

I felt a sudden surge of hatred for my brother – a bitterness I'd never felt so strongly before. How did he get to be so perfect and talented – and I got to have dyspraxia? It wasn't fair.

I came out of the loo and slipped into the music room opposite, switching on the light. Jamie's violin case was lying against the wall. I opened it quietly and pulled out the bow, running my hand up and down its smooth wooden edge. With venom and the strength of all my frustration and rage, I snapped it in half against my leg. Crack. I hadn't expected it to give so easily – and felt a moment of shock. What had I done? That bow was valuable – Jamie loved it. But my anger returned. So what?

I slipped quietly back to my room, leaving the two snapped pieces on the floor. Frantically but as silently as I could, I began stuffing clothes into a bag. I didn't know what I was going to do – where I was going. I knew I had to go – I had to get away. I wasn't wanted here.

I put on my jacket and crept downstairs, unlocking the front door carefully, so as not to make a noise. The door clicked open and I closed it very slowly. There was hardly a sound. It was so bitterly cold outside I nearly had second thoughts – but something in me made me keep walking. The direction didn't matter – I didn't care where I ended up. I zipped my jacket as high as it would go and pulled on my gloves.

By the time I reached the main road, my ears were

stinging with cold. Looking up the road, I saw that a bus was coming. I ran for the stop and held out my hand. The bus hissed to a halt. I hadn't noticed the number. I didn't care. It would take me away from here – and much faster and warmer than if I walked. I reached into my pocket, suddenly realising how little money I had on me. At least there was enough for a bus fare.

I paid and sat down, dazed, as the bus set off. Mum and Dad's words kept playing over and over in my head. 'Needs special teaching.' 'Boarding school.' Tears pricked my eyes again.

I looked out of the window as the bus turned a corner. It was heading down Masterton Road. It must be the 623 – or the equivalent night bus. I was heading towards the place I'd been two days before – Craig's house – the house of the murderer.

Without having time to think it over, I pressed the bell and got off at Craig's stop. The cold wind brushed harshly against my face. I felt like it was saying no – turn back. I shivered. The bus pulled away. I walked, still on a kind of auto-pilot, towards Craig's road and down to Number Seven. I stood outside his house and looked at it. Only then did I begin to ask myself what I was doing there. It was pointless. What did I think I was going to do – ring the bell? Check out my theory with him? Why hadn't I stayed on the bus in the warm?

The house was dark apart from a light on in the front room upstairs. The curtains were drawn but they were only thin material and the light shone through. I was about to walk away, when I caught a sudden glimpse of a shadow moving behind the curtain. Or was it two people? I wasn't sure straight away but then the shadows separated – definitely two people. I tensed. Was I imagining it – or from their frenzied movements against the window – were they fighting? Maybe they were being passionate? No – I was sure one was hitting the other. That's what it looked like. There was a noise – a thud – as if something had been thrown against a wall. Then a scream – a woman's scream – I was sure.

I looked round – terrified, willing a light to come on in one of the neighbouring houses. Surely someone had heard. No light came on. They were all in darkness. It felt like a dream – a nightmare. Maybe if I pinched myself I'd wake up. I tried. 'Ouch!' I was definitely awake. What was going on? Could it be Craig up there – killing again?

I gulped. I couldn't take the risk. I couldn't let another woman die because I hadn't done something. I pulled off my right glove, and grabbed my mobile from my pocket, my hands shaking. I glanced up at the window. Shapes still moving – but further from the window. I couldn't see. I pressed 999.

'Police,' I said, when I was asked which service. I was put through quickly.

'Please, I think someone's being murdered,' I said. 'They're fighting – it's Number Seven, Chestnut Close, Thurbridge Hill. You'd better come quick – and get an ambulance too. The woman's screaming.'

She was. I could hear her again.

'Don't worry, son – we're on our way.'

I felt a surge of relief but that quickly turned to panic as I looked up at the window. They were still fighting, I could see from the shadows. Then the woman seemed to disappear. There was no more screaming. I had a sudden horrific thought. Could it be *Danielle*? Was Craig up there killing Danielle?

The man – the one who'd been stalking her – could it be Craig? Maybe he was the 'boyfriend' she was going out with yesterday. He could have given a false name – it was possible, wasn't it? It was still quiet. Whoever the woman was, maybe she was too hurt to scream. Maybe she was dead – or dying. How long were the police going to take? It might be too long. I had to do something more.

I grabbed a stone from the path and threw it up towards the window. It missed by a mile and fell without even hitting the wall. I found another, a smaller one – moved closer to the house, and aimed. Yes – it hit the window. But had Craig heard?

I looked up – the curtain had been pulled aside. The window was opening. It was Craig – sticking his head out.

'Oy – you! What d'you think you're bloody doing?'

I turned and ran. But he must have been running too – down the stairs, out into the street, because I was only a few doors down when I heard a door bang. He was after me. He was coming after me. This was what I'd wanted – to create a diversion – to stop him hitting Danielle, but now I'd done it, it felt like a mistake. Why hadn't I waited for the police? What if he caught up with me? I hadn't thought about him chasing me, only about stopping the fight.

Why hadn't I run back the way I came, back towards the main road? I didn't know where Chestnut Close came out. Chestnut *Close* – with horror I realised this meant it didn't come out, it was a dead end. I could hear the man's footsteps. He was gaining on me. I'm not a fast runner.

He's going to kill me, I thought.

Why had I come here? Why hadn't I gone to the police sooner? Danielle – if anything had happened to her it would be my fault – all my fault. The Close was long, it curved round a corner – and then, suddenly I could see the end. I'd had it.

But then I noticed – in the light of the streetlamp – there was a gap between the two end houses, with a metal barrier to stop people riding bikes through. I swung through it, the metal bar knocking hard against me, but I didn't dare slow down. Ahead it was very black – no lights. What was it – a field?

The man was so close behind, almost near enough to grab me.

'Oy! Stop, you bastard!' he yelled.

I was still running – but suddenly there was nothing under my feet. After the briefest second of total panic, I hit icy water with a massive splash. Shock. Like falling through ice. The canal! I was in the canal. The water was biting cold – agonising. My heavy jacket and jeans pulled me down. I couldn't swim – no way. I couldn't swim with heavy clothes on and the cold and the man...

I went under, came up, took a spluttering breath and was under again. I flung my arms about, desperately trying to remember what Danielle had said about treading water. Drawing small circles with my arms. Just stay afloat – stay calm, keep your head above the water, I told myself. And I was doing it! I was doing it! My arms must be doing it right because I was staying up – just about. But how long for? I knew I couldn't keep it up for long. Another voice inside my head was saying, you're going to drown. You're going to die.

Then I heard a voice shouting. Was it Craig? I couldn't make out the words. The voice came again. There was a splash. Was he coming in after me?

'Get hold of the ring!' I heard it this time – a man's voice – and at the same moment caught sight of an orange and white lifebelt, floating towards me.

I reached for it – but missed, went under and came up gasping. This time I managed to grab it. And kicked my heavy legs towards the bank.

Arms reached down and yanked me up, my body twisting painfully. I lay, coughing, gasping, shivering uncontrollably on the bank, water spurting from my mouth.

Someone had a torch. Rubbing my eyes, I could see two policemen leaning over me. I tried to speak but it was a while before I could get any words out.

'Did you...did you...did you get him?' I said hoarsely, my teeth chattering. 'Craig – did you get him?'

'Yes, don't you worry – we've got him.'

I heaved a sigh of relief. Then the fear returned. 'Danielle...' I croaked. 'Is she all right?'

'Who?'

'Danielle...' My voice had gone hoarse again. 'He was killing her – upstairs in the house – Craig's house.'

The policeman didn't answer straight away. She's dead, I thought. He's not telling me because she's dead. I'd been too late – too late.

I began to cry big exhausted tears. Someone put a blanket round me.

'He...he...he killed Neeta Gupta,' I sobbed, 'and ...and now Danielle. She's my cousin – Danielle – my cousin...she was.'

'Hey, hey, calm down. I'm not sure what you're on about,' said a policeman. 'Let's see if you can sit up. There, that's better.'

I sat up, still shaking and sobbing. But the world was spinning. I threw up.

Chapter 28

The policeman drove me home. He held the car door open as I stumbled out of the police car, the blanket still round me. Then he rang the doorbell. We waited. The light came on in the hallway. The front door opened and there was Dad, in his pyjamas. His dazed, sleepy expression changed to one of alarm when he saw us.

'*What on earth?*'

At that moment Mum appeared on the stairs in her dressing gown.

'Who is it? What's going on?' she demanded.

'Your son was being chased and he ended up in the canal,' the policeman explained. 'He's cold and wet but none the worse for wear apart from that. Will you bring him to the station in the morning? We'd like him to make a statement.'

'Yes – of course,' said Dad, rubbing his eyes.

The policeman left. I began to shiver.

Dad was standing staring at me and I knew he was going to start asking questions any moment. I didn't want to talk about it – any of it – not now.

'I do...don't understand,' he stuttered. 'What on earth were you doing out at this time of night?'

I was silent. Mum pushed Dad aside. She touched my face. 'He's frozen,' she gasped, and pulled off the blanket.

'Get upstairs, Michael, and under the shower,' she

told me. 'I'll put the kettle on and make you a hot chocolate.'

Upstairs, I closed the bathroom door behind me with relief.

Clean and warm after the shower, I slipped into my bedroom and snuggled under the duvet.

'Better?' asked Mum, coming in. She turned on the bedside light and put down a mug of hot chocolate. I still had the taste of canal in my mouth – the hot chocolate was tempting. I sat up. Mum perched on the edge of the bed.

Then Dad came in. He stood at the foot of the bed. Jamie was behind him, hovering in the doorway.

I felt a sense of dread.

'So,' said Dad. 'What exactly were you up to?'

'Please,' I begged. 'Can I tell you about it in the morning? I'm shattered – I need to sleep.'

'Yes – let him sleep,' said Mum. 'We can talk tomorrow.'

'I want to know now,' Dad insisted. 'I've been woken up in the middle of the night by the police with my son and I want to know what it's all about. What were you doing out at this time of night?'

'I...I was running away,' I said quietly.

'*You were what?*'

'Running away from home,' I said. 'I know you don't want me here.'

'What do you mean?' said Mum. 'Of course we want you.'

I shook my head. 'You were planning to send me away. I heard you – you can't deny it.' I felt my muscles tightening at the memory of what I'd heard.

174

'Send you away?' said Dad. 'What are you talking about?'

'To a special school – I heard you say it.' Tears began to slip down my face. I was crying – I couldn't stop myself.

'Oh, Michael,' said Mum, gasping with realisation. 'You've misunderstood.'

'No – I h-h-h-heard you – I know I did.'

'They weren't talking about you, you twerp,' said Jamie, quietly. He came towards the bed. 'It was me. I asked Mum and Dad if I could go to Goodwins School – it's a specialist music school.'

'*You?*' I stared at him in disbelief. 'You want to go to *boarding* school?'

Jamie nodded but he didn't meet my eyes. 'Martin and Sam from the Youth Orchestra go there. It's too far away so I'd have to board – but I don't think I'd mind that.'

I wiped my eyes. What was this about?

'I thought you liked it at our school. You said the music department is really good.'

Jamie's shoulders were visibly tensing. It was his turn to look as if he was going to cry. He said nothing.

'Why, Jamie?' I pressed. 'I don't understand.'

'If you must know,' he said, suddenly beginning to sob, 'I hate it at Thurbridge High. I hate it. I hate it. I *hate* it.

'You hate it?' said Mum, her eyes wide with surprise. 'You never said. We thought you were getting on well.'

'Getting on well isn't everything,' Jamie said quietly, 'not when certain people are determined to make your

175

life a misery – just 'cos you're different – 'cos you've got a talent and they haven't and they hate you for it.'

Mum looked distressed. 'Who's been making your life a misery?' she asked. 'And why haven't you told us?'

'Freddy Finch and his gang,' said Jamie. 'They've been bullying me since last term. I thought I could handle it – stay out of their way. Then this term it got a lot worse. They started demanding money. If I didn't pay up, they said they'd break my violin.'

'Why on earth didn't you tell us?' Dad asked. 'We could have done something to help.'

'They said if I told … they'd break my fingers, one by one. They said they'd make sure I'd never play the violin again – and they meant it. I know they did.'

Jamie turned, sobbing and walked out of the room. Mum went after him.

Dad and I were silent. I tried to take it all in. Mum and Dad weren't sick of me – they weren't planning to send me away. The relief of this almost set me off crying again. And Jamie – he was being bullied by Freddy Finch. All those snide looks from Sean suddenly made sense. He knew – of course he did. And the phone calls – the heavy breathing – it must've been him trying to wind me up – or maybe Freddy wanting to scare Jamie. And Jamie hadn't told me anything. Did he really think I wouldn't have helped him? I thought guiltily about the broken bow in the music room. Jamie didn't know about that yet. I was going to be paying out from my pocket money for a long time.

'Will you let him go to Goodwins?' I asked Dad.

'We'll see. He'll have to apply for a scholarship – I

don't think we could afford the full fees. But whatever happens about that we'll definitely make sure that something is done about those bullies. Demanding money with menaces – that's a criminal offence. I expect they'll be excluded at the very least. If only Jamie had come to us earlier.'

A sudden thought flashed through my head. The money – the money Mum had accused me of taking – it must have been Jamie. And he'd let me take the blame. For a moment I felt better about breaking his bow but it didn't last. Freddy had threatened to break Jamie's violin. I'd broken his bow. I was nearly as bad as the bullies. I'd thought everything was perfect for Jamie but it wasn't. Having a talent didn't mean he didn't have problems too.

'I thought we were an open kind of family,' said Dad, sighing. 'I thought if either of you had a problem, you would tell us.'

I lay back on the pillow. Dad didn't know the half of it about me yet...

Chapter 29

It was the next day. Still dazed and confused, I found myself sitting in an interview room in the local police station. Dad sat, looking spaced out, by my side and a policeman and policewoman sat opposite.

I was suddenly aware that still no one had told me about Danielle. It must be because Craig killed her. Otherwise why hadn't they said?

'Danielle?' I asked. 'Please – why won't anyone tell me if she's okay?'

Dad turned sharply to look at me. 'What's Danielle got to do with all this?' he asked.

I said nothing but looked at the policeman and woman – trying to read their faces. They looked confused – as if they didn't know what I was talking about.

The policewoman leaned forward. 'Who is this Danielle? Why do you think something's happened to her?'

I found myself babbling. 'She's my cousin and she was being stalked. I'm sure it was Craig stalking her. He killed Neeta Gupta and Danielle was at the same university. Craig must've found out that Danielle was nosing around, asking questions about Neeta – trying to find out what happened. He knew she knew his name. She was doing it for me – I asked her to see what she could find out. Craig didn't know that though. He must've wanted to shut her up. That's why he was

attacking her last night – Danielle – wasn't he? You can
tell me – even if it's bad news – I need to know. I should
have warned her – but I'd only just worked it out...'

'Slow down,' said the policeman, holding up his hands.
'Last night, Craig was attacking his mother – that's what
you saw. Her name's not Danielle. It's Brenda.'

'His mother?' I repeated in surprise. 'It wasn't
Danielle?'

'No. Craig's mother saw him going after you down
the road,' the policeman explained. 'It was her who told
us and that's how we found you in the canal. Those night
duty officers were luckily only two streets away in their
car. It looks like you probably saved her life – or saved
her from serious injury at any rate. You did well, calling
us and distracting him when you did. Then she helped
you out too.'

'Is she all right?' I asked.

'Badly bruised but all right apart from that. They
didn't keep her in at the hospital.'

'Now,' said the policewoman impatiently, 'you said
that Craig Benson murdered Neeta Gupta. What makes
you think that?'

I could feel my knees knocking together under the table.
'I saw.'

The words came out before I could think straight. Dad
turned sharply, his eyes widening in disbelief.

'You witnessed Craig murdering Neeta Gupta?' the
policeman repeated.

'No – no, I didn't see him actually murder her. I saw
them fighting by the canal – that afternoon – the day it
happened.'

179

'But you didn't contact the police at the time?'

'No, I didn't think it was that serious. I didn't know he was going to murder her, did I?'

'But the next day,' said the policeman, 'when you heard about it – why didn't you come forward then?'

'I felt bad. If I'd told someone straight away what I saw, then maybe she would still be alive. And I didn't see him close up – only his back – so I didn't think I'd be much use as a witness.'

'You only saw his back?'

I nodded.

'Then how are you so sure it was Craig?'

'I recognised his voice . . . ' I began.

'You knew him then?'

'No – he was shouting, like, by the canal – and I recognised his voice in the street the other day.'

The policeman and policewoman both looked doubtful.

'And I've got other evidence too,' I added. 'I know his motive and everything.'

The policeman cocked his head on one side. 'You do, do you?'

I nodded. 'Honest.'

'So if you had all this evidence, why didn't you bring it to us? What were you doing hanging about outside Craig's house at midnight last night?'

'I was going to come today. I had to tell Shamila first. She's Neeta's cousin and she's in my class at school. I thought we could come together and tell you. You see, she's got the photo and the bus ticket.'

'The photo and the bus ticket?' said the policewoman.

I took a deep breath and explained in detail all the clues and my theory about Craig's scam and how I'd come to be there last night. Dad sat silently beside me, his knuckles tapping on the table the whole time.

'Do you think I got it right?' I asked when I'd finished. 'I mean, it's only a theory…'

'We'll certainly have to look into it,' said the policeman.

Chapter 30

I'm sitting on a wooden bench in the hallway of the courtroom, waiting. It's July now and baking hot. My clothes are sticking to me. They've got a fan going but it's not helping much.

Dad's sitting next to me and Craig's mum's opposite. She's looking pale. I'm feeling bad enough – I can't imagine how she's feeling. She thanked me though, for turning up at her house when I did. Apparently Craig had been staying with her since he got thrown out of his flat for not paying the rent. He had gambling debts and had people on his back – people he owed money to. He was sponging off her; he'd even taken money from her handbag.

She said he'd been a complete nightmare to live with. He'd kept asking her for money but he already owed her loads. She'd put her foot down – refused to lend him any more. She said she'd first become suspicious when she'd come in to see Craig watching *Crimewatch* on TV. He switched channels the instant he saw her but not before she saw what it was about – Neeta's death. If he hadn't changed channels she wouldn't have thought anything of it, but when she thought about it she realised Craig had disappeared for a few days just when Neeta went missing. Since he'd come back he'd been behaving all angry and agitated.

She didn't want to believe it but the more she thought

about it the more she thought Craig must have been involved. For days after that she considered going to the police. But she didn't like the idea of dobbing in her own son and she wasn't completely sure, so she decided to ask him straight out. She'd hoped if he admitted it that she could persuade him to turn himself in.

It was a crazy thing to do. For some reason she never imagined he'd get violent – not to her, his mother. He'd treated her badly – called her all sorts, but he'd never hit her before. It was a total shock when he started laying into her.

'Michael.'

I turn in surprise because it's Shamila and she's saying my name. She hasn't spoken to me since she found out the truth – what I knew – what I'd seen that day by the canal. I've tried umpteen times to talk to her – to explain – but she'll never listen. She always walks away. Until now.

Now she's come up to me deliberately and said my name. Her mum sits down on the same side as Craig's mum and Shamila sits down near me but further along the bench, away from other people. She beckons to me with a jerk of the head. I shuffle along to sit beside her.

'Hi,' I say awkwardly.

She speaks quietly. 'I thought you might not be here,' she says. 'I thought you'd bottle out and not turn up.'

I'm indignant. 'Of course I'm here.'

I have to be here. I have to stand up and be questioned as a witness – the only witness to the fight between Neeta and Craig.

There's an awkward silence for a moment. Is that all she's come to say – to tell me she thought I'd bottle out? But she's sitting here beside me – this is my chance – my chance to say the things I've been wanting to say for so long. I might not get another. I search desperately for the words.

'I'm sorry,' I say – and I immediately cringe, it sounds so crass.

She's looking at the floor, twiddling her hair.

'I know I messed things up big time,' I continue. 'I know I should have done something, said something – it just got harder and harder as time went on. D'you see? I hope you can forgive me.'

Her face is stony. She is silent. I wish I could find the words to make it all okay. But I can't.

'He'll go down,' I tell her. 'Manslaughter if not murder. He'll go to prison for a long time.'

'I hope so,' she says.

I feel sick about what Craig did but at the same time I can't help feeling a glow deep inside because my theory was right. I *had* worked it out – before the police were anywhere near solving the case. They have since found two other women who Craig had tried to 'borrow' money from, with his made-up sob story about his little girl having cancer. Neither of them had actually given him money.

At least it wasn't Craig who was stalking my cousin Danielle. How lucky was I that her stalker turned out to be a wimpy guy from Uni who had a crush on her?

'Do the police know how they first met?' I ask. 'Craig and Neeta – I've always wondered . . . '

Shamila shakes her head. 'They don't know for sure – but it looks like they met at a café on Drummond Street. D'you know it?'

184

'No.'

'It's round the backstreets – not very near the Uni. The police found a guy who works there who recognised Craig's photo. He remembers seeing them together a few times. We know Neeta was finding it hard settling in as a student. I think she went there rather than the Uni canteen to get away – find a bit of space that wasn't full of students. Craig must've been there too and spotted her – on her own, looking vulnerable. The police think he may have noticed her coat and thought she had money.'

Shamila's voice has gone wobbly. I can see her hands are shaking.

'Look – maybe it's better not to talk about it,' I say. 'I don't want to upset you.'

'It's okay. I've got to talk about it soon, haven't I – in that courtroom? I've got to tell them about the photo of Amy.'

She wipes her moist brow and pushes her hair back from her face as if in an effort to pull herself together.

'It was an expensive coat,' she continues. 'My mum told her she should wear something studenty – to fit in more but she loved that grey cashmere coat. She insisted on wearing it. If only she hadn't worn it...'

Shamila sniffs. 'I'm scared, Michael. Aren't you scared? To stand there in court – with *him* there too.'

'Yeah,' I admit, 'a bit.'

Actually I'm scared as hell.

'But you could be in another room if you want,' I tell her, 'with a video link. Didn't they say?'

'I know – they did say that. But in a way, even though it's scary I want to do it – to stand there in that courtroom.'

I nod.

'I hoped he'd just admit it – plead guilty,' says Shamila. 'Then we wouldn't have to go through all this. I can't believe he was going to deny even knowing Neeta.'

'Yeah – but he's not anymore, is he?'

'That's right,' she says. 'The police found one red thread in his jacket pocket. It's an exact match with the Indian scarf Neeta was wearing when she died.'

'Amazing what they can do now,' I say, 'forensics and that. There's quite a lot of evidence when you put it all together. Don't worry – I'm sure he'll go down. And once the court case is over, at least you can move on.'

'*Move on!*' she snaps. 'It's not as easy as that, Michael. You have no idea what grief is like.'

'Sorry,' I say, shrinking back from her. 'I just meant it'll be a relief – you know, once it's finished and he's gone to prison. I hoped – I hope we might be friends again.'

'*Friends?*' she sneers. 'After what you did – or what you didn't do, more like?'

'Sorry,' I say again. 'It's too soon – I know.'

I meet the daggers in her eyes. 'It'll always be too soon, Michael – always.'

With that she stands up and goes to sit with her mum. I feel my heart sinking into my shoes as I shuffle back along next to Dad. I look over at Shamila from time to time but she won't meet my eyes. I'm thinking – thinking about everything. I'm not sure how much time passes. I am vaguely aware of Shamila walking off through the swing doors towards the toilets.

Then suddenly, Dad's tapping me on the shoulder. I turn. I've been sitting here in a world on my own and haven't heard my name being called.

'Calling Michael Emmerson! Calling Michael Emmerson!'

Dad squeezes my hand as I stand up shakily.

'Don't worry, you'll be fine,' he says. 'Just tell the truth and speak up clearly.'

'I will,' I tell him.

I take a deep breath and I walk towards the open door of the courtroom.